SWISS COTTAGE
STRAND

THE
AROUND THE WORLD
TREASURES:

BLACK BEAUTY

THE
AROUND THE WORLD
TREASURES:
GREAT BRITAIN

BLACK BEAUTY

BY ANNA SEWELL

PICTURES BY
CHARLES MOZLEY

FRANKLIN WATTS, INC., NEW YORK
MAYFLOWER PUBLISHING CO. LTD, LONDON

This book was designed and produced by Rainbird,
McLean Ltd, 11 Charlotte Street, London, W.1. The
text, color plates and jackets were printed by J. H.
de Bussy N.V., Amstèrdam, Holland. The paper was
supplied by Corvey N.V., Amsterdam. The binding
is by Van Rijmenam N.V., The Hague, Holland.

FIRST PRINTING 1959

Library of Congress Catalog Number 59-11158

About this Book

ANNA SEWELL, who was born in England in 1820, spent her early years in a poor section of London. From the time Anna could understand words, her mother told her stories of the country and brought her up to understand that animals – particularly horses – have feelings and should be treated with love and kindness.

In a period when all traffic was pulled by horses, Anna saw animals brutally mistreated. With horror she watched overloaded carts sliding down on to the horses pulling them. She saw exhausted horses being beaten as they dragged coal carts over the slippery cobbles. She would watch, her nose pressed to a window, as hackney-carriage horses waited hour after hour in rain or sleet for a fare, and she suffered with them.

At her grandfather's farm, on the other hand, Anna had a chance to ride horseback and to see horses well treated. When she was twelve her parents moved to a former coach house where the old harness was still hanging, and where she could piece together the history of the horses who had been stabled there.

Two years later, running home from school to get out of a storm, Anna slipped and badly twisted both ankles. Probably she did not receive proper medical attention, for she was a cripple from that day onward. Now from being a doer Anna was forced to become a listener. It must have been very hard for her, for she had a violent temper and a jealous streak that did not make it easy for her to watch others enjoying themselves when she could not.

Her family moved several more times. Anna was delighted when they moved to a house in the country, where she could have a pony and carriage. There are no words to describe what that pony meant to Anna. He allowed her to come and go as she wished, just like other people. He made it easier for her to talk to people, for a horse helps to break down barriers. And, thanks to that pony, Anna's ear was able to record the talk of ostlers, grooms, and stable boys, which was later to help make BLACK BEAUTY such an outstanding book.

In 1857 she went by herself to Germany to visit a doctor who might cure her ankles. He could not cure them entirely, but for a time they were so much better that Anna was able to walk a little and – joy of joys – to ride horseback.

Meanwhile, Anna's mother had become a professional writer; one of her poems, "Mother's Last Words", sold over a million copies, and others of her verses sold extraordinarily well. When Anna returned from Germany, she began to help her mother in preparing her verses for the press, and in correcting proof.

When Anna was fifty-one, she knew that she was at the beginning of her last illness and would never go out again. Her first concern was for her old pony. She found him a happy home where others would love him as much as she had. Then she settled down to what looked like a life of complete invalidism.

But she wrote in her journal: "I am writing the life of a horse." Anna was so ill that the book took five years to write. At times, she could not hold a pen but dictated the story to her mother.

BLACK BEAUTY was published late in 1877. The reviews rolled in, and everyone praised her. By the following April, the book had sold 90,000 copies and Anna was famous.

Anna died that same April. But BLACK BEAUTY has never died.

Horses play an important part in the lives of most people in Britain. There are horse shows all over the country which families for miles around attend. Also, in London on the Monday after Whit Sunday there is a special show for working horses – those who draw the milk carts, brewers' drays, and the costers' barrows – just the type of horse in fact that in Anna Sewell's day so often was cruelly treated. Such horses now have no need of defenders, for they are cherished friends of their owners, and loved by the public. Recently when a mare unexpectedly foaled in a London street, people came running from every house carrying coats and rugs to keep the mother and child warm, until a horse ambulance arrived.

Horse riding, at one time exclusively an amusement of the rich, is now within the reach of all, for there are inexpensive riding clubs on the outskirts of most cities, and at horse shows the competitors come from every walk of life.

In this wonderful change in less than a hundred years BLACK BEAUTY has played a large part. The book is widely known, for not only is it in all children's libraries, but is a school reader. In fact so popular is it with British children that in many homes BLACK BEAUTY does not seem a fictional character, but as much part of the family as their pet cat or dog. Wouldn't Anna Sewell be pleased?

Noel Streatfeild

The Picture Story of
Black Beauty

2. The first place I can well remember was a large meadow.

3. One morning my master got on my back and rode me around the meadow. It certainly did feel queer; but I must say I felt rather proud to carry my master.

4. A man came from Squire Gordon's, and took me away to the Hall. I lived some years with Squire Gordon.

5. The next time Ginger and I were together in the paddock,
she told me about her first place.

6. At last, after a terrible struggle Ginger threw him off over her head.

7. Sometimes the Vicarage children used to come and play with Miss Jessie and Flora.

8. As for Ginger and me, our greatest pleasure was when we were saddled for a riding party, the master on Ginger, the mistress on me, and the young ladies on Sir Oliver and Merrylegs.

9. One day late in the autumn, my master had a long
   journey to make. There had been a great deal of rain,
   and now the wind was very high.

10. It was wonderful what a number of places
master would go to in the city on Saturday,
and what queer streets we went through.

11. The head ostler of the principal hotel was a pleasant, active little man.

12. "The fire engine! The fire engine!" shouted two or three
voices, and clattering and thundering over the stones two
horses dashed into the yard with the heavy engine
behind them.

13. The next day Joe came to the stables to learn all he could before James left.

14. John rang the bell twice, and then knocked at the door
like thunder.

15. Master came down, carrying the mistress in his arms.

16. Earlshall was a very fine house. Two footmen were standing ready dressed in livery, with scarlet breeches and white stockings. Presently my lady came down the stone steps.

17. My lady's hat was gone and her long brown hair was streaming behind her. Her head and body were thrown back, as if she were pulling with all her remaining strength.

18. I was a "job horse" and was let out to all sorts of people who wished to hire me. As I was good-tempered and gentle, I think I was oftener let out to the ignorant drivers than some of the other horses.

19. A policeman walked in, holding the child tight by the
arm. The boy looked very frightened and began to cry;
but there was no escape, and he led the way to the cornbin.

20. I was sold at a horse fair, with hundreds of other horses.

21. We journeyed on steadily until we reached
    the city. The lamps were already lighted.

22. Alongside the railings a number of cabs were drawn up,
waiting for passengers.

23. A young man, carrying a heavy suitcase, stepped on a
piece of orange peel, which lay on the sidewalk, and
fell down with great force.

24. "Oh, very well," said the gentleman. "Don't trouble
yourself any further, Mr. Barker. I will enquire somewhere else."

25. When my harness was taken off, I did not know what
I should do first – eat the grass, or roll over on my back,
or lie down and rest, or have a gallop across the meadow
out of sheer spirits at being free.

26. When the streets were slippery with frost or snow, that was the worst of all for us horses. One mile of such going with a weight to draw and no firm footing, would take more out of us than four on a good road.

27. One day a shabby old cab drove up beside ours. The
    horse was an old worn-out chestnut, with an ill-kept
    coat, and bones that showed plainly through it. The
    knees knuckled over, and the forelegs were very unsteady.

28. Jerry helped the young woman out and rang the bell.

29. He was whipping me cruelly, when a lady stepped quickly up to him and said in a sweet earnest voice, "Please do not whip your good horse any more!"

30. I shall never forget my new master; he had black eyes
and a hooked nose, his mouth was as full of teeth as a
bulldog's and his voice was as harsh as the grinding of
cart wheels over gravel. His name was Nicholas Skinner.

31. I noticed a man who looked like a gentleman-farmer, with a young boy by his side.

32. A very stately-looking person was Miss Blomefield, the
younger lady – Miss Ellen – took to me very much.

Black Beauty

1. My Early Home

THE first place that I can well remember was a large
pleasant meadow with a pond of clear water in it. Some
shady trees leaned over it, and rushes and water lilies
grew at the deep end. Over the hedge on one side we
looked into a field, and on the other we looked over a
gate at our master's house, which stood by the roadside;
at the top of the meadow was a plantation of fir trees,
and at the bottom a running brook overhung by a steep
bank.

While I was young I lived upon my mother's milk, as
I could not eat grass. In the daytime I ran by her side, and
at night I lay down close by her. When it was hot, we
used to stand by the pond in the shade of the trees, and
when it was cold, we had a nice warm shed near the
plantation.

As soon as I was old enough to eat grass, my mother
used to go out to work in the daytime, and came back in
the evening.

There were six young colts in the meadow besides me;
they were older than I was; some were nearly as large
as grown-up horses. I used to run with them, and had
great fun; we used to gallop all together around and
around the field, as hard as we could go. Sometimes we
had rather rough play, for they would frequently bite and
kick as well as gallop.

One day, when there was a good deal of kicking, my
mother whinnied to me to come to her, and then she said:

"I wish you to pay attention to what I am going to say
to you. The colts who live here are very good colts, but
they are cart horse colts, and, of course, they have not

learned manners. You have been well bred and well born; your father has a great name in these parts, and your grandfather won the cup two years at the Newmarket races; your grandmother had the sweetest temper of any horse I ever knew, and I think you have never seen me kick or bite. I hope you will grow up gentle and good, and never learn bad ways; do your work with a good will, lift your feet up well when you trot, and never bite or kick even in play."

I have never forgotten my mother's advice; I knew she was a wise old horse, and our master thought a great deal of her. Her name was Duchess, but he often called her Pet.

Our master was a good, kind man. He gave us good food, good lodging, and kind words; he spoke as kindly to us as he did to his little children. We were all fond of him, and my mother loved him very much. When she saw him at the gate, she would neigh with joy, and trot up to him. He would pat and stroke her and say, "Well, old Pet, and how is your little Darkie?" I was a dull black, so he called me Darkie; then he would give me a piece of bread, which was very good, and sometimes he brought a carrot for my mother. All the horses would come to him, but I think he liked us best. My mother always took him to the town on a market day in a little gig.

There was a farm boy, Dick, who sometimes came into our field to pick blackberries from the hedge. When he had eaten all he wanted, he would have what he called fun with the colts, throwing stones and sticks at them to make them gallop. We did not much mind him, for we could gallop off; but sometimes a stone would hit and hurt us.

One day he was at this game, and did not know that the master was in the next field; but he was there, watching what was going on: over the hedge he jumped in a snap, and catching Dick by the arm, he gave him a heavy blow on the ear that made him roar with the pain and surprise. As soon as we saw the master, we trotted up nearer to see what went on.

"Bad boy!" he said, "bad boy! to chase the colts. This is not the first time, nor the second, but it shall be the last. There – take your money and go home, I shall not want you on my farm again." So we never saw Dick any more. Old Daniel, the man who looked after the horses, was just as gentle as our master, so we were well off.

2. The Hunt

BEFORE I was two years old, something happened which I have never forgotten. The other colts and I were feeding at the lower part of the field when we heard in the distance, what sounded like the cry of dogs. The oldest of the colts raised his head, pricked his ears, and said, "There are the hounds!" and immediately cantered off, followed by the rest of us, to the upper part of the field, where we could look over the hedge and see several fields beyond. My mother and an old horse were also standing near, and seemed to know all about it.

"They have found a hare," said my mother, "and if they come this way, we shall see the hunt."

And soon the dogs were all tearing down the field next to ours. I never heard such a noise as they made. They kept on a "yo! yo, o, o! yo! yo, o, o!" at the top of their voices. After them came a number of men on horseback, some of them in green coats, all galloping às fast as they could. The old horse looked eagerly after them, and we young colts wanted to be galloping with them, but they were soon away into the fields lower down. Here it seemed as if they had come to a stand; the dogs left off barking, and ran about every way with their noses to the ground.

But before long the dogs began their "yo! yo, o, o!" again, and back they came all together at full speed, making straight for our meadow at the part where the high bank and hedge overhung the brook.

"Now we shall see the hare," said my mother; and just then a hare wild with fright rushed by, and made for the plantation. On came the dogs, they burst over the bank, leaped the stream, and came dashing across the field, followed by the huntsmen. Six or eight men leaped their horses over, close upon the dogs. The hare tried to get through the fence, but it was too late. The dogs were upon her with their wild cries; we heard one shriek, and that was the end of her. One of the huntsmen rode up and whipped off the dogs. He held her up by the leg, torn and bleeding, and all the gentlemen seemed well pleased.

As for me, I was so astonished that at first I did not see what was going on by the brook, but when I did look, there was a sad sight. Two fine horses were down, one was struggling in the stream, and the other was groaning on the grass. One of the riders was getting out of the water covered with mud – the other lay quite still.

"His neck is broken," said my mother.

"And serve him right too," said one of the colts.

I thought the same, but my mother did not agree.

"Well! no," she said, "you must not say that; but I never yet could make out why men are so fond of this sport.

They often hurt themselves, often spoil good horses, and tear up the fields – and all for a hare or a fox, or a stag, that they could get more easily some other way, but we are only horses, and don't know."

My master, who had been watching what was going on, was the first to raise the young man. His head fell back and his arms hung down, and everyone looked very serious. There was no noise now. Even the dogs were quiet, and seemed to know that something was wrong. They carried him to our master's house. I heard afterwards that it was young George Gordon, the Squire's only son, a fine, tall young man, and the pride of his family.

There was now riding off in all directions – to the doctor's, to the farrier's, and no doubt to Squire Gordon's, to let him know about his son. When the farrier came to look at the black horse that lay groaning on the grass, he shook his head; one of his legs was broken. Then some one ran to our master's house and came back with a gun. Presently there was a loud bang and a dreadful shriek, and then the black horse moved no more.

My mother seemed much troubled. She said she had known that horse for years, and that his name was "Rob Roy". He was a good bold horse, and there was no vice in him. She never would go to that part of the field again.

Not many days after, we heard the church bell tolling for a long time; and looking over the gate we saw a long strange black coach that was covered with black cloth and was drawn by black horses. After that came another and another and another, and all were black, while the bell kept tolling, tolling. They were carrying young Gordon to the churchyard to bury him. He would never ride again. What they did with Rob Roy I never knew – but it was all for one little hare.

3. My Breaking In

I WAS now beginning to grow handsome; my coat had grown fine and soft, and was bright black. I had one white foot, and a pretty white star on my forehead. My master would not sell me until I was four years old; he said lads ought not to work like men, and colts ought not to work like horses until they were quite grown up.

When I was four years old, Squire Gordon came to look at me. He examined my eyes, my mouth, and my legs, and then I had to walk and trot and gallop before him. He seemed to like me, and said, "When he has been well broken in, he will do very well." My master said he would break me in himself, as he should not like me to be frightened or hurt, and he lost no time about it, for the next day he began.

Every one may not know what breaking in is, therefore I will describe it. It means to teach a horse to wear a saddle and bridle and to carry on his back a man, woman, or child; to go just the way they wish and to go quietly. Besides this, he has to learn to wear a collar, a crupper, and a breeching, and to stand still while they are put on; then to have a cart or a chaise fixed behind him, so that he cannot walk or trot without dragging it after him. And he must go fast or slow, just as the driver wishes. He must never start at what he sees, nor speak to other horses, nor bite, nor kick, nor have any will of his own, but always do his master's will, even though he may be very tired or hungry. But the worst of all is, when his harness is once on, he may neither jump for joy nor lie down for weariness. So you see this breaking in is a great thing.

I had of course long been used to a halter and a head-stall, and to being led about in the field and lanes quietly, but now I was to have a bit and a bridle. After a good deal of coaxing, my master got the bit into my mouth, and the bridle fixed, but it was an unpleasant thing! Those who have never had a bit in their mouths cannot think how bad it feels; a great piece of cold hard steel as thick as a man's finger to be pushed into your mouth, between your teeth and over your tongue, with the ends coming out at the corner of your mouth, and held fast there by straps over your head, under your throat, around your nose, and under your chin; so that no way in the world can you get rid of the cold hard thing. It is very bad! yes, very bad! at least I thought so; but I knew all horses wore them when they were grown up. And so, what with the nice oats, and what with my master's pats, kind words, and gentle ways, I got to wear my bit and bridle.

Next came the saddle, but that was not half so bad. My master put it on my back very gently, while old Daniel held my head. He then made the girths fast under my body, patting and talking to me all the time, then I had a few oats, then a little leading about. This he did every day until I began to look for the oats and the saddle. At length, one morning my master got on my back and rode me around the meadow. It certainly did feel queer – but I must say I felt rather proud to carry my master, and as he continued to ride me a little every day, I soon became accustomed to it.

The next unpleasant business was putting on the iron shoes. That too was very hard at first. My master went with me to the smith's forge, to see that I was not hurt or frightened. The blacksmith took my feet in his hands one after the other, and cut away some of the hoof. It did not pain me. Then he took a piece of iron the shape of my foot, and clapped it on, and drove some nails through the shoe right into my hoof, so that the shoe was firmly on. My feet felt very stiff and heavy, but in time I got used to it.

And now, having got so far, my master went on to break me to harness; there were more new things to wear. First, a stiff heavy collar just on my neck, and a bridle with great side-pieces against my eyes called blinkers, so that I could not see on either side, but only straight in front of me. Next, there was a small saddle with an unpleasant stiff strap that went right under my tail; that was the crupper. To have my long tail doubled up and poked through that strap was almost as bad as the bit. I never felt more like kicking, but of course I could not kick such a good master, and so in time I got used to everything, and could do my work as well as my mother.

I must not forget to mention one part of my training, which I have always considered a very great advantage. My master sent me for some days to a nearby farmer's, who had a meadow which was skirted on one side by the railway. Here were some sheep and cows, and I was turned in among them.

I shall never forget the first train that ran by. I was feeding quietly near the railings which separated the meadow from the railway, when I heard a strange sound at a distance, and before I knew from where it came – with a rush and a clatter, and a puffing out of smoke – a long black train of something flew by, and was gone almost before I could draw my breath. I turned, and galloped to the further side of the meadow as fast as I could go. In the course of the day many other trains went by, some more slowly. These drew up at the station close by, and sometimes made an awful shriek and groan before they stopped. I thought it very dreadful, but the cows went on eating very quietly, and hardly raised their heads as the frightening black thing came puffing and grinding past.

For the first few days I could not eat in peace; but as I found that this terrible creature never came into the field, or did me any harm, I began to disregard it, and very soon I cared as little about the passing of a train as the cows and sheep did.

To this day, thanks to my good master's care, I am as fearless at railway stations as in my own stable.

My master often drove me in double harness with my mother, because she was steady and could teach me best. She told me that it was wisest always to do my best to please my master. "But," said she, "there are a great many kinds of men; there are good, thoughtful men like our master, that any horse may be proud to serve – but there are also bad, cruel men, who never ought to have a horse or dog to call their own. There are a great many foolish men, as well, who never trouble themselves to think; these spoil more horses than all, just for want of sense. I hope you will fall into good hands; but a horse never knows who may buy him, or who may drive him. Do your best, wherever it is, and keep up your good name."

44

4. Birtwick Park

EARLY in May, a man came from Squire Gordon's, and took me away to the Hall. My master said, "Good-bye, Darkie; be a good horse, and always do your best." I could not say "good-bye", so I put my nose into his hand; he patted me kindly, and I left my first home.

As I lived some years with Squire Gordon, I may as well tell something about the place. Squire Gordon's Park skirted the village of Birtwick. It was entered by a large iron gate, at which stood the first lodge, and then you trotted along on a smooth road between clumps of large old trees; then another lodge and another gate which brought you to the house and the gardens. Beyond this lay the home paddock, the old orchard, and the stables. There was room for many horses and carriages; but I need only describe the stable into which I was taken; this was very roomy, with four good stalls; a large swinging window opened into the yard, which made it pleasant and airy.

The first stall was the largest and shut in behind with a wooden gate. It had a low rack for hay and a low manger for corn. It was called a loose box, because the horse that was put into it was not tied up, but left loose, to do as he liked. It is a great thing to have a loose box.

Into this fine box the groom put me. It was clean, sweet and airy and I could see all that went on through the iron rails that were at the top.

He gave me some very nice oats, and then went away.

When I had eaten my oats I looked around. In the stall next to mine stood a little fat gray pony, with a thick mane and tail, a very pretty head, and a pert nose.

I said, "How do you do? what is your name?"

He said, "My name is Merrylegs. I carry the young ladies on my back, and sometimes I take our mistress out in the low chair. They think a great deal of me, and so does James. Are you going to live next door to me in the box?"

I said "Yes".

"Well then, "he said, "I hope you are good-tempered; I do not like any one next door who bites."

Just then a horse's head looked over from the stall beyond; the ears were laid back, and the eye looked rather ill-tempered. This was a tall chestnut mare, with a long handsome neck. She looked across to me and said:

"So it is you who have turned me out of my box; it is a very strange thing for a colt like you, to come and turn a lady out of her own home."

"I beg your pardon," I said, "the man who brought me put me here, and I had nothing to do with it; and as to being a colt, I am turned four years old, and am a grown-

46

up horse. I never had words yet with horse or mare, and it is my wish to live at peace."

"Well", she said, "we shall see. Of course I do not want to have words with a young thing like you." I said no more.

In the afternoon when we went out, Merrylegs told me all about it:

"Ginger has a bad habit of biting and snapping – that is why they call her Ginger. And when she was in the loose box, she used to snap very much. One day she bit James in the arm and made it bleed, and so Miss Flora and Miss Jessie, who are very fond of me, were afraid to come into the stable. They used to bring me nice things to eat, an apple or a carrot, or a piece of bread, but with Ginger in that box, they dare not come, and I miss them very much. I hope they will now come again, if you do not bite or snap."

I told him I never bit anything and could not think what pleasure Ginger found in it.

"Well, I don't think she does find pleasure," said Merrylegs. "It is just a bad habit; she says no one was ever kind to her, and why should she not bite? but I am sure, if all she says is true, she must have been very ill-used before she came here. John and James do all they can to please her, and our master never uses a whip if a horse acts right; so I think she might be good-tempered here. You see," he said with a wise look, "I am twelve years old. I know a great deal, and I can tell you there is not a better place for a horse all around the country than this. John is the best groom that ever was, he has been here fourteen years; and you never saw such a kind boy as James is, so that it is all Ginger's own fault that she did not stay in that box."

5. A Fair Start

THE name of the coachman was John Manly. He had a wife and one little child, and they lived in the coachman's cottage, very near the stables.

The next morning he took me into the yard and gave me a good grooming, and just as I was going into my box with my coat soft and bright, the Squire came in to look at me, and seemed pleased. "John," he said, "you may as well take him on a round after breakfast. Go by the common and the Highwood, and back by the watermill and the river – that will show his paces."

After breakfast John came and fitted me with a bridle. He was very particular in letting out and taking in the straps, to fit my head comfortably. Then he brought the saddle, and as that was not broad enough for my back, he went for another, which fitted nicely. He rode me first slowly, then at a trot, then a canter, and when we were on the common he gave me a light touch with his whip, and we had a splendid gallop.

"Ho, ho! my boy," he said, as he pulled me up, "you would like to follow the hounds, I think."

As we came back through the Park we met the Squire and Mrs. Gordon walking; they stopped, and John jumped off.

"Well, John, how does he go?"

"Splendidly, sir," answered John. "He is as fleet as a deer, and has a fine spirit too; but the lightest touch of the rein will guide him. Down at the end of the common we met one of those carts hung all over with baskets, rugs, and such like; you know, sir, many horses will not pass those carts quietly; he just took a good look at it, and then went on as quiet and pleasant as could be. They were shooting rabbits near the Highwood, and a gun went off close by; he pulled up a little and looked, but did not stir a step to right or left. It's my opinion he has not been frightened or ill-used while he was young.'

"That's well," said the Squire. "I will try him myself to-morrow."

The next day I was brought up for my master. I found

he was a very good rider, and thoughtful for his horse too. When we came home the lady was at the hall door as he rode up.

"Well, my dear," she said, "how do you like him?"

"He is exactly what John said," he replied. "A pleasanter creature I never wish to mount. What shall we call him?"

"He is really quite a beauty, and he has such a sweet good-tempered face and such a fine intelligent eye – what do you say to calling him Black Beauty?"

"Black Beauty – why, yes, I think that is a very good name. If you like, it shall be his name." And so it was.

When John went into the stable, he told James that master and mistress had chosen a good sensible English name for me, that meant something, not like Marengo, or Pegasus, or Abdallah. They both laughed, and James said, "I might have named him Rob Roy, for I never saw two horses more alike."

"That's no wonder," said John, "didn't you know that Farmer Grey's old Duchess was the mother of them both?"

So poor Rob Roy who was killed at that hunt was my brother! I did not wonder that my mother was so troubled. It seems that horses have no relations; at least, they never know each other after they are sold.

John seemed very proud of me. He used to make my mane and tail almost as smooth as a lady's hair, and he would talk to me a great deal. I grew very fond of him. He was so gentle and kind, he seemed to know just how a horse feels, and when he cleaned me, he knew the tender places, and the ticklish places; when he brushed my head, he went as carefully over my eyes as if they were his own.

James Howard, the stable boy, was just as gentle and pleasant in his way, so I thought myself well off.

A few days after this I had to go out with Ginger in the carriage. I wondered how we would get on together but except for laying her ears back when I was led up to her, she behaved very well. She did her work honestly, and I never wish to have a better partner in double harness. When we came to a hill, instead of slackening her pace, she would throw her weight right into the collar, and pull away straight up. John had oftener to hold us in, than to urge us forward; he never had to use the whip with either of us. Our paces were much the same, and I found it very easy to keep step with her when trotting, which made it pleasant, and master always liked it when we kept step well, and so did John. After we had been out two or three times together we grew quite friendly and sociable.

As for Merrylegs, he and I soon became great friends. He was such a cheerful, plucky, good-tempered little fellow that everyone liked him and especially Miss Jessie and Flora, who used to ride him about in the orchard.

Our master had two other horses in another stable. One was Justice, a roan cob, used for riding, or for the luggage cart. The other was an old brown hunter, named Sir Oliver. He was past work now, but the master was very fond of him and gave him the run of the Park. He sometimes pulled some light carts on the estate, or carried one of the young ladies when they rode out with their father; for he was very gentle, and could be trusted with a child as well as Merrylegs. The cob was a strong, well-made, good-tempered horse, and we sometimes had a little chat in the paddock, but of course I could not be so intimate with him as with Ginger, who stood in the same stable.

6. Liberty

I WAS quite happy in my new place but I missed my liberty. For three years and a half of my life I had had all the liberty I could wish for; but now, week after week, month after month, and no doubt year after year, I must stand up in a stable night and day except when I was wanted, and then I must be just as steady and quiet as any old horse who has worked twenty years. Straps here and straps there, a bit in my mouth, and blinkers over my eyes. Now, I am not complaining, for I know it must be so. I only mean to say that for a young horse full of strength and spirits who has been used to some large field, where he can fling up his head, and toss up his tail and gallop away at full speed – I say it is hard never to have liberty to do as he likes. Sometimes, when I had had less exercise than usual, I felt so full of life and spring that when John took me out to exercise, I really could not keep quiet. Do what I would, it seemed as if I must jump, or dance, or prance – and many a good shake I know I must have given him, especially at the first. But he was always good and patient.

"Steady, steady, my boy," he would say. "Wait a bit, and we'll have a good swing, and soon get the tickle out of your feet." Then as soon as we were out of the village he would give me a few miles at a brisk trot, and then bring me back as fresh as before, but clear of the fidgets, as he called them. Spirited horses, when not enough exercised, are often called skittish, when it is only play and some grooms will punish them; but our John did not – he knew it was only high spirits. Still, he had his own ways of making me understand by the tone of his voice or the touch of the rein. If he was very serious and quite determined, I always knew it by his voice, and that had more power with me than anything else, for I was very fond of him.

I ought to say that sometimes we had our liberty for a few hours. This used to be on fine Sundays in the summer-time. The carriage never went out on Sundays, because the church was not far off.

It was a great treat for us to be turned out into the Home Paddock or the old orchard. The grass was so cool and soft to our feet, the air so sweet, and the freedom to do as we liked so pleasant, we could gallop, lie down, and roll over on our backs, or nibble the sweet grass. Then it was a very good time for talking, as we stood together under the shade of the large chestnut tree.

7. Ginger

ONE day I told Ginger about my training.

"Well," said she, "if I had had your bringing up I might have had as good a temper as you have, but now I don't believe I ever shall."

"Why not?" I said.

"Because it has all been so different with me," she replied. "I never had any one, horse or man, that was kind to me. I was taken from my mother as soon as I was weaned, and put with a lot of other young colts. The man that had the care of us never gave me a kind word in my life. I do not mean that he ill-used me, but he did not care for us one bit other than seeing that we had plenty to eat and shelter in the winter.

"A footpath ran through our field, and very oftent he great boys passing through would fling stones to make us gallop. I was never hit, but one fine young colt was badly cut in the face. Of course it made us more wild, and we decided that boys were our enemies.

"We had very good fun in the free meadows, galloping up and down and chasing each other around and around the field, then standing still under the shade of the trees. But when it came to breaking in, several men came to catch me. When at last they closed me in at one corner of the field, one caught me by the forelock; another caught me by the nose, and held it so tight I could hardly draw my breath; then another took my under jaw in his hard hand and wrenched my mouth open – and so by force they got on the halter and the bar into my mouth. Then one dragged me along by the halter, another whipping behind, and this was the first experience I had of men's kindness. It was all force; they did not give me a chance to know what they wanted. I was highbred and had a great deal of spirit, and was very wild, no doubt, and gave them plenty of trouble. But then it was dreadful to be shut up in a stall day after day instead of having my liberty, and I fretted and pined and wanted to get loose. You know yourself, it's bad enough when you have a kind master and plenty of coaxing.

"There was one – the old master – who could have done anything with me, but he had given up all the hard part of the trade to his son and to another experienced man, and he only came at times to oversee. His son was a strong, tall, bold man. They called him Samson, and he used to boast that he had never found a horse that could throw him. There was no gentleness in him as there was in his father, but only hardness. I felt from the first that what he wanted was to wear all the spirit out of me, and just make me into a quiet, humble, obedient piece of horseflesh. 'Horseflesh!' Yes, that is all that he thought about!" And Ginger stamped her foot as if the very thought of him made her angry.

She went on: "If I did not do exactly what he wanted, he would get put out, and make me run around with that long rein in the training field until he had tired me out. He drank a good deal, and I am quite sure that the oftener he drank, the worse it was for me. One day he had worked me hard in every way he could, and when I laid down I was tired and miserable and angry; it all seemed so hard. The next morning he came for me early, and ran me around again for a long time. I had scarcely had an hour's rest, when he came again for me, with a saddle and bridle and a new kind of bit. He had only just mounted me on the training ground, when something I did put him out of temper, and he chucked me hard with the rein. The new bit was very painful, and I reared up suddenly, which angered him still more, and he began to whip me. I felt my whole spirit set against him, and I began to kick, and plunge, and rear as I had never done before. For a long time he stuck to the saddle and punished me cruelly with his whip and spurs, but my blood was thoroughly up, and I cared for nothing he could do if only I could get him off. At last, after a terrible struggle, I threw him off over my head. I heard him fall heavily on the turf, and without looking behind me, I galloped off to the other end of the field; there I turned around and saw my persecutor slowly rising and going into the stable.

"I stood under an oak tree and watched, but no one came to catch me. The time went on, the sun was very hot, the flies swarmed round me, and settled on my bleeding flanks where the spurs had dug in. I felt hungry, for I had not eaten since the early morning, but there was not enough grass in that meadow for a goose to live on. I wanted to lie down and rest, but with the saddle strapped tightly on, there was no comfort, and there was not a drop of water to drink. The afternoon wore on, and the sun got low. I saw the other colts led in, and I knew they were having a good meal.

"At last, just as the sun went down, I saw the old master come out with a sieve in his hand. He was a very fine old gentleman with white hair, but his voice was what I should know him by anywhere. It was full, and clear, and kind, and when he gave orders everyone knew, both horses and men, that he expected to be obeyed. He came quietly along, now and than shaking the oats about that he had in the sieve, and speaking cheerfully and gently to me. 'Come along, lassie, come along, lassie. Come

along, come along.' I stood still and let him come up. He held the oats to me and I began to eat without fear; his voice took all my fear away. He stood by, patting and stroking me while I was eating, and seeing the clots of blood on my side he seemed very vexed. 'Poor lassie! it was a bad business, a bad business!' Then he quietly took the rein and led me to the stable. Just at the door stood Samson. I laid my ears back and snapped at him. 'Stand back,' said the master, 'and keep out of her way; you've done a bad day's work for this filly.' He growled out something about a vicious brute. 'A bad-tempered man will never make a good-tempered horse,' said the father. 'You've not learned your trade yet, Samson.' Then he led me into my box, took off the saddle and bridle and tied me up. Then he called for a pail of warm water and a sponge, took off his coat, and while the stable man held the pail, he sponged my sides so tenderly that I was sure he knew how sore and bruised they were. 'Whoa! my pretty one,' he said. 'Stand still, stand still.' His very voice did me good, and the bathing was very comfortable. The skin was so broken at the corners of my mouth that I could not eat the hay, the stalks hurt me. He looked closely at it, shook his head, and told the man to mix a good bran mash and put some meal into it. How good that mash was! and so soft and healing to my mouth. He stood by all the time I was eating, stroking me and talking to the man. 'If a high spirited creature like this,' said he, 'can't be broken in by fair means, she will never be good for anything.'

"After that he often came to see me, and when my mouth was healed, the other breaker, Job they called him, went on training me. He was steady and thoughtful, and I soon learned what he wanted."

8. Ginger's Story Continued

THE next time that Ginger and I were together in the paddock, she told me about her first place. "After my breaking in," she said, "I was bought by a dealer to match another chestnut horse. For some weeks he drove us together, and then we were sold to a fashionable gentleman, and were sent up to London. I had been driven with a bearing rein by the dealer, and I hated it worse than anything else; but in this place we were reined far tighter, the coachman and his master thinking we looked more stylish so. We were often driven about in the Park and other fashionable places. You, who never had a bearing rein on, don't know what it is, but I can tell you it is dreadful.

"I like to toss my head about, and hold it as high as any horse – but fancy now yourself, if you were obliged to hold it there, and that for hours on end, not able to move it at all, except with a jerk still higher, your neck aching until you did not know how to bear it. Beside that, you have two bits instead of one – and mine was a sharp one, it hurt my tongue and my jaw, and the blood from my tongue reddened the froth that kept flying from my lips, as I chafed and fretted at the bits and rein. It was worse when we had to stand by the hour waiting for our mistress at some grand party. If I fretted or stamped with impatience the whip was laid on. It was enough to drive one mad."

"Did not your master take any thought for you?" I said.

"No," said she, "he only cared to have a stylish turn-out, as they call it; I think he knew very little about horses, he left that to his coachman, who told him I was irritable, but should soon get used to it. But *he* was not the man to do it, for when I was in the stable, miserable and angry, instead of being soothed and quieted by kindness, I got only a surly word or a blow. If he had been civil, I would have tried to bear it. I was willing to work hard, but to be tormented for nothing but their fancies angered me. What right had they to make me suffer like that? Besides the soreness in my mouth and the pain in my neck, it always made my windpipe feel bad, and if I had stayed there long, I know it would have spoiled my breathing. But I grew more and more restless and irritable, I could not help it; and one day, just after they had buckled us into the carriage, and were straining my head up with that rein, I began to plunge and kick with all my might. I soon broke a lot of harness, and kicked myself clear – so that was an end of that place.

"After this, I was sent to Tattersall's to be sold; of course I could not be warranted free from bad habits, so nothing was said about that. My handsome appearance and good paces soon got me sold to another dealer; he tried me in all kinds of ways, with different bits and without a bearing rein and soon found out what I could bear. At last he sold me as a perfectly quiet horse to a gentleman in the country. He was a good master, and I was getting on very well, but his old groom left him and a new one came. This man was as brutal as Samson; he always spoke in a rough, impatient voice, and if I did not move in the stall the moment he wanted me, he would hit me above the hocks with his stable broom or the fork. I hated him; he wanted to make me afraid of him, but I was too high spirited for that and one day I bit him, which of course put him in a great rage, and he began to hit me about the head with a riding whip. After that, he never dared to come into my stall again. Either my heels or my teeth were ready for him, and he knew it. I was quite quiet with my master, but of course he listened to what the man said, and so I was sold again.

"The same dealer heard of me, and said he thought he knew one place where I should do well.' 'Twas a pity,' he said, 'that such a fine horse should go to the bad, for want of a real good chance,' and I came here not long before you did; but by then I had made up my mind that men were my natural enemies and that I must defend myself. Of course it is very different here, but who knows how long it will last? I wish I could think about things as you do but I can't after all I have gone through."

"Well," I said, "I think it would be a real shame if you were to bite or kick John or James."

"I don't mean to," she said, "while they are good to me. I did bite James once pretty badly, but John said, 'Try her with kindness,' and instead of punishing me as I expected, James came to me with his arm bound up, and brought me a bran mash and stroked me and I have never snapped at him since, and I won't either."

I was sorry for Ginger, but I found that as the weeks went on, she grew much more gentle and cheerful, and lost her watchful, defiant look. One day James said, "I do believe that mare is getting fond of me. She, quite whinnied after me this morning when I had been rubbing her forehead."

"Aye, aye, Jim," said John, "she'll be as good as Black Beauty by and by; kindness is all the tonic she wants, poor thing!" Master noticed the change too, and one day when he got out of the carriage and came to speak to us as he often did, he stroked her beautiful neck, "Well, my pretty one, how do things go with you now? You are a good bit happier than when you came to us, I think."

She put her nose up to him in a friendly, trustful way, while he rubbed it gently.

"We shall make a cure of her, John," he said.

"Yes, sir, she's wonderfully improved, it's the Birtwick balls, sir," said John, laughing.

This was a little joke of John's; he used to say that a regular course of the Birtwick horse-balls would cure almost any vicious horse; these balls, he said, were made up of patience and gentleness, firmness and petting, one pound of each to be mixed up with half-a-pint of common sense, and given to the horse every day.

9. Merrylegs

MR. BLOMEFIELD, the Vicar, had a large family; sometimes they used to come and play with Miss Jessie and Flora. When they came, there was plenty of work for Merrylegs, for nothing pleased them so much as getting on him and riding him all about the orchard and the home paddock, and this they would do for hours.

One afternoon he had been out with them a long time, and when James brought him in and put on his halter, he said:

"There, you rogue, mind how you behave yourself, or we shall get into trouble."

"What have you been doing, Merrylegs?" I asked.

"Oh!" said he, tossing his little head, "I have only been giving those young people a lesson. They did not know when they had had enough, nor when I had had enough, so I just pitched them off backwards, that was the only thing they could understand."

"What?" said I, "you threw the children off? I thought you knew better than that! Did you throw Miss Jessie or Miss Flora?"

He looked very much offended, and said:

"Of course not! I would not do such a thing for the best oats that ever came into the stable. Why, I am as careful of our young ladies as the master could be, and as for the little ones, it is I who teach them to ride. When they seem frightened or a little unsteady on my back, I go as smooth and as quiet as old pussy when she is after a bird; so don't you trouble yourself preaching to me. I am the best friend and the best riding master those children have. It is not them, it is the boys. Boys," said he, shaking his mane, "are quite different; they must be broken in, as we were broken in when we were colts, and must be taught what's what. The other children had ridden me about for nearly two hours, and then the boys thought it was their turn, and so it was, and I was quite agreeable. They rode me by turns, and I galloped them about up and down for a good hour. They had each cut a great hazel stick for a riding whip, and laid it on a little too hard; but I took it in good part, until at last I thought we had had enough, so I stopped two or three times by way of a hint. Boys, you see, think a horse or pony can go on as long and as fast as they please. They never think that a pony can get tired, or have any feelings, so, as the one who was whipping me could not understand, I just rose up on my hind legs and let him slip off behind. Then the other boy got up, and as soon as he began to use his stick I laid him on the grass – and so on, until they were able to understand. They are not bad boys, they don't wish to be cruel. I like them well enough but you see, I had to give them a lesson. When they brought me to James and told him, I think he was very angry to see such big sticks."

"If I had been you," said Ginger, "I would have given those boys a good kick, and that would have taught them a lesson."

"No doubt you would," said Merrylegs, "But then I am not quite such a fool (begging your pardon) as to anger our master or make James ashamed of me. Besides, those children are under my charge when they are riding. Why, only the other day I heard our master say to Mrs. Blomefield, 'My dear madam, you need not be anxious about the children, my old Merrylegs will take as much care of them as you or I could; he is so perfectly good-tempered and trustworthy'. Do you think I am such an ungrateful brute as to forget all the kind treatment I have had here for five years, and all the trust they place in me, and turn vicious because a couple of ignorant boys used me badly? No! no! you never had a good place where they were kind to you, and so you don't know. I wouldn't vex our people for anything; I love them," said Merrylegs.

"Besides," he went on, "if I took to kicking, where would I be? Why, sold off in a jiffy, and no character, and I might find myself slaved about under a butcher's boy, or worked to death at some place where no one cared for me, except to find out how fast I could go, or whipped along in some cart with three or four great men in it going out for a Sunday spree. No," said he, shaking his head, "I hope I shall never come to that."

10. A Talk in the Orchard

GINGER and I were not of the regular tall carriage horse breed; we had more of the racing blood in us. We stood about fifteen and a half hands high; we were therefore just as good for riding as we were for driving, and our master used to say that he disliked either horse or man that could do but one thing. As for us, our greatest pleasure was when we were saddled for a riding party, the master on Ginger, the mistress on me, and the young ladies on Sir Oliver and Merrylegs. It was so cheerful to be trotting and cantering all together, that it always put us in high spirits. I had the best of it, for I always carried the mistress. Her weight was little, her voice was sweet, and her hand was so light on the rein, that I was guided almost without feeling it.

Oh! if people knew what a comfort to horses a light hand is, and how it keeps a good mouth and a good temper, they surely would not drag and pull at the rein as they often do. Our mouths are so tender, that where they have not been spoiled or hardened with bad or ignorant treatment, they feel the slightest movement of the driver's hand, and we know in an instant what is required of us. My mouth had never been spoiled, and I believe that was why the mistress preferred me to Ginger, although her paces were certainly quite as good. She often used to envy me, and said it was all the fault of breaking in, and the gag bit in London, that her mouth was not so perfect as mine; and then old Sir Oliver would say, "There, there! don't vex yourself. You have the greatest privilege, a mare that can carry a tall man of our master's weight, with all your spring and sprightly action, does not need to hold her head down because she does not carry the lady. We horses must take things as they come, and always be contented and willing so long as we are kindly used."

I had often wondered how it was that Sir Oliver had such a very short tail; it really was only six or seven inches long, with a tassel of hair hanging from it; and on one of our holidays in the orchard I ventured to ask him by what accident it was that he had lost his tail.

"Accident!" he snorted, with a fierce look, "it was no accident! it was a cruel, shameful, cold-blooded act! When I was young I was taken to a place where cruel things were done; and they cut off my long beautiful tail, through the flesh, and through the bone, and took it away."

67

"How dreadful!" I exclaimed.

"Dreadful! ah! it was dreadful. But it was not only the pain, though that was terrible and lasted a long time. It was not only the indignity of having my best ornament taken from me, though that was bad; but it was this, how could I ever brush the flies off my sides and my hind legs any more? You who have tails just whisk the flies off without thinking about it, and you can't tell what a torment it is to have them settle upon you and sting and sting, and have nothing in the world to lash them off with. I tell you it is a lifelong wrong, and a lifelong loss; but thank Heaven! they don't do it now."

"What did they do it for then?" said Ginger.

"For fashion!" said the old horse, with a stamp of his foot. "There was not a well-bred young horse in my time that did not have his tail docked in that shameful way, just as if the good God that made us did not know what we wanted and what looked best."

"I suppose it is fashion that makes them strap our heads up with those horrid bits that I was tortured with in London," said Ginger.

"Of course it is," said he. "To my mind, fashion is one of the wickedest things in the world. Now look, for instance, at the way they treat dogs – cutting off their tails to make them look smart, and shaving up their ears to a point to make them look sharp. I had a dear friend once, a brown terrier – called Skye; she was so fond of me that she made her bed under my manger, and there she had a litter of five as pretty little puppies as could be. None were drowned, for they were a valuable kind, and how pleased she was with them! and when they got their eyes open and crawled about, it was a real pretty sight. But one day the man came and took them all away. I thought he might be afraid I should tread upon them. But it was not so; in the evening poor Skye brought them back again, one by one in her mouth; not the happy little things that they had been, but bleeding and crying pitifully. They had all had a piece of their tails cut off, and the soft flap of their pretty little ears. They healed in time and they forgot the pain, but the nice soft flap that of course was intended to protect the delicate part of their ears from dust and injury was gone for ever. Why don't they cut their own children's ears into points to make them look sharp? Why don't they cut the ends off their noses to make them look smart? One would be just as sensible as the other. What right have they to torment and disfigure God's creatures?"

What Sir Oliver said was all so new to me and so dreadful that I found a bitter feeling towards men rise up in my mind that I had never had before. Of course Ginger was much excited; she flung up her head with flashing eyes, and distended nostrils, declaring that men were both brutes and blockheads.

"Who talks about blockheads?" said Merrylegs, who had just come up from the old apple tree, where he had been rubbing himself against the low branch. "I believe that is a bad word."

"Bad words were made for bad things," said Ginger, and she told him what Sir Oliver had said. "It is all true," said Merrylegs, sadly, "but you know that master, and John, and James are always good to us, and talking against men in such a place as this doesn't seem fair or grateful, and you know there are good masters and good grooms besides ours, though of course ours are the best." This wise speech of good little Merrylegs, which we knew was quite true, cooled us all down, specially Sir Oliver, who was dearly fond of his master; and to turn the subject I said, "Can any one tell me the use of blinkers?"

'No!' said Sir Oliver, shortly, 'because they are no use.'

"They are supposed," said Justice in his calm way, "to prevent horses from shying and starting and getting so frightened as to cause accidents."

"Then what is the reason they do not put them on riding horses – especially on ladies' horses?" said I.

"There is no reason at all," said he quietly, "except the fashion; they say that a horse would be so frightened to see the wheels of his own cart or carriage coming behind him, that he would be sure to run away, although of course when he is ridden, he sees them all about him if the streets are crowded. I admit they do sometimes come too close to be pleasant, but we don't run away, we are used to it, and understand it, and if we never had blinkers put on, we should never want them; we should see what was there, and know what was what, and be much less frightened than by only seeing bits of things that we can't understand."

Of course there may be some nervous horses who have been hurt or frightened when they were young, and may be the better for them, but as I never was nervous, I can't judge.

"I consider," said Sir Oliver, "that blinkers are dangerous things in the night. We horses can see much better in the dark than man can, and many an accident would never have happened if horses might have had the full use of their eyes. Some years ago, I remember, there was a hearse with two horses returning one dark night, and just by farmer Sparrow's house, where the pond is close to the road, the wheels went too near the edge, and the hearse was overturned into the water. Both the horses were drowned, and the driver only just escaped. If those horses had not been partly blinded, they would of themselves have kept farther from the edge, and no accident would have happened. When our master's carriage was overturned, before you came here, it was said that if the lamp on the left side had not gone out, John would have seen the great hole that the road makers had left – and so he might. But if old Colin had not had blinkers on, he would have seen it, lamp or no lamp, for he was far too knowing an old horse to run into danger. As it was, he was very much hurt, the carriage was broken, and how John escaped nobody knew."

"I should say," said Ginger, curling her nostril, "that these men, who are so wise, had better give orders that in future all foals should be born with their eyes set just in the middle of their foreheads, instead of on the side."

Things were getting rather sore again, when Merrylegs said, "I'll tell you a secret; I believe John does not approve of blinkers; I heard him talking with master about it one day. The master said that if horses had been used to them, it might be dangerous in some cases to leave them off. John said he thought it would be a good thing if all colts were broken in without blinkers, as was the case in some foreign countries. So cheer up, and let us run to the other end of the orchard; I believe the wind has blown down some apples, and we might just as well eat them as the slugs."

Merrylegs could not be resisted, so we broke off our long conversation, and got up our spirits by munching some very sweet apples which lay scattered on the grass.

11. Plain Speaking

THE longer I lived at Birtwick, the more proud and happy I felt at having such a place. Our master and mistress were respected and beloved by all who knew them. They were good and kind to everybody and everything. There was no oppressed or ill-used creature that had not a friend in them, and their servants took the same tone. If any of the village children were known to treat any creature cruelly, they soon heard about it from the Hall.

The Squire and Farmer Grey had worked together, as they said, for more than twenty years, to get bearing reins on the cart horses done away with, and in our parts we seldom saw them; but sometimes if mistress met a heavily laden horse, with his head strained up, she would stop the carriage and get out, and reason with the driver and try to show him how foolish and cruel it was.

I don't think any man could resist our mistress. I wish all ladies were like her. Our master too used to come down very heavy sometimes. I remember he was riding me towards home one morning, when we saw a powerful man driving towards us in a light pony chaise, with a beautiful little bay pony, with slender legs, and a highbred sensitive head and face. Just as he came to the Park gates, the little thing turned towards them. The man, without word or warning, wrenched the creature's head around with such force and suddenness, that he nearly threw it on its haunches. Recovering itself, it was going on, when he began to lash it furiously. The pony plunged forward, but the strong heavy hand held the pretty creature back with force almost enough to break its jaw and lashed it with the whip.

"Sawyer," cried master in a stern voice, "is that pony made of flesh and blood?"

"Flesh and blood and temper," he said. "He's too fond of his own will." He spoke as if he was in a strong passion; he was a builder who had often been to the Park on business.

"And do you think," said master sternly, "that treatment like this will make him fond of your will?"

"He had no business to make that turn; his road was straight on!" said the man roughly.

"You have often driven that pony up to my place," said master. "It only shows the creature's memory and intelligence; how did he know that you were not going there again? But that has little to do with it. I must say, Mr. Sawyer, that more unmanly, brutal treatment of a little pony I never saw, and by giving way to such passions you injure your own character as much as you injure your horse, and remember, we shall all have to be judged by our works, towards man or towards beast."

Master rode me home slowly, and I could tell by his voice how the thing had grieved him. He was just as free to speak to gentlemen of his own rank, for another day, when we were out, we met a Captain Langley, a friend of our master's, driving a splendid pair of grays. After a little conversation the Captain said:

"What do you think of my new team, Mr. Gordon? you know you are the judge of horses in these parts, and I should like your opinion."

The master backed me a little, so as to get a good view of them. "They are an uncommonly handsome pair," he said, "and if they are as good as they look, I am sure you need not wish for anything better; but I see you still hold to that pet scheme of yours for worrying your horses and lessening their power."

"You mean the bearing reins?" said the other. "Oh, I know that's a hobby of yours but I like to see my horses hold their heads up."

"So do I," said master. "But I don't like to see them *held up*; that takes all the shine out of it. Now you are a military man, Langley, and no doubt like to see your regiment look well on parade, 'Heads up,' and all that; but you would not take much credit for your drill if all your men had their heads tied to a backboard! It might not be much harm on parade, except to worry and fatigue them, but how would it be in battle, when they want the free use of every muscle, and all their strength thrown forward? It is just the same with horses; you fret and worry their tempers, and decrease their power. You will not let them throw their weight against their work, and so they have to do too much with their joints and muscles, and of course it wears them faster. You may depend upon it, horses were intended to have their heads free, as free as men's are; and if we could act a little more according to common sense, and a good deal less according to fashion, we should find many thing work easier. Besides you know as well as I that, if a horse makes a false step, he has much less chance of recovering himself if his head and neck are fastened back. And now," said the master, laughing, "I have given my hobby a good trot out; can't you make up your mind to mount him too, Captain? your example would go a long way."

"I believe you are right in theory," said the other, "and that's rather a hard hit about the soldiers, but – well – I'll think about it," and so they parted.

12. A Stormy Day

ONE day late in the autumn, my master had a long journey to make. I was put into the dogcart, and John went with his master. I always liked to go in the dogcart, it was so light, and the high wheels ran along so pleasantly. There had been a great deal of rain, and now the wind was very high, and blew the dry leaves across the road in a shower. We went along merrily until we came to the toll-gate, and the low wooden bridge. The bridge, was so low in the middle, that if the river was full, the water would be nearly up to the woodwork and planks. But as there were good substantial rails on each side, people did not mind it.

The man at the gate said the river was rising fast, and he feared it would be a bad night. Many of the meadows were under water, and in one low part of the road the water was halfway up to my knees. The bottom was good, and master drove gently, so it did not matter.

As the master's business engaged him a long time, we did not start for home until rather late in the afternoon. The wind was then much higher, and I heard the master say to John, he had never been out in such a storm; and so I thought, as we went along the edge of a wood, where the great branches were swaying about like twigs, and the rushing sound was terrible.

"I wish we were well out of this wood," said my master.

"Yes, sir," said John, "it would be rather awkward if one of these branches came down upon us."

The words were scarcely out of his mouth, when there was a groan, and a crack, and a splitting sound, and crashing down among the other trees came an oak, torn up by the roots, and it fell right across the road just before

us. I will never say I was not frightened, for I was. I stopped still, and I believe I trembled; of course, I did not turn around or run away; I was not brought up to do that. John jumped out and was at my head in a moment.

"That was a very near thing," said my master. "What's to be done now?"

"Well, sir, there is nothing to do but to go back to the four crossroad, and that will be a good six miles before we get around to the wooden bridge again. It will make us late, but the horse is fresh."

So back we went, and around by the crossroads. By the time we got to the bridge it was very nearly dark. We could just see that the water was over the middle of it; but as that had happened before, master did not stop. We were going along at a good pace, but the moment my feet touched the bridge, I knew there was something wrong and stopped dead. "Go on, Beauty," said my master, and he gave me a touch with the whip, but I did not stir. He gave me a sharp cut, I jumped, but I dared not go forward.

"There's something wrong sir," said John, and he sprang out of the dogcart and came to my head and looked all about. He tried to lead me forward. "Come on, Beauty, what's the matter?" Of course I could not tell him, but I knew very well that the bridge was not safe.

Just then the man at the tollgate on the other side ran out of the house, tossing a torch about like a madman.

"Stop!" he cried.

"What's the matter?" shouted my master.

"The bridge is broken in the middle and part of it is carried away; if you come on you'll be into the river."

"Thank God!" said my master. "You Beauty!" said John, and took the bridle and gently turned me around to the other road. The sun had set some time, the wind seemed to have died down. I trotted quietly along, the wheels hardly making a sound on the soft road. For a good while neither master nor John spoke, and then master began in a serious voice. I learned that, if I had gone on as the master wanted me, most likely the bridge would have given way under us, and we would all have fallen into the river; and as the current was flowing very strongly, and it was nearly dark, it was more than likely we would all have been drowned. Master said God had given men reason, but He had given animals knowledge which did not depend on reason, and which was much more prompt and perfect in its way, and by which they had often saved the lives of men. John had many stories to tell of dogs and horses, and the wonderful things they had done; he thought people did not value their animals half enough, nor make friends of them as they ought to do. I am sure he made friends of them if ever a man did.

At last we came to the Park gates, and found the gardener looking out for us. He said that mistress had been in a dreadful way ever since dark, fearing some accident had happened. We saw a light at the hall door and at the upper windows, and as we came up mistress ran out, saying, "Are you really safe, my dear? Oh! I have been so anxious. Have you had an accident?"

"No, my dear; but if Black Beauty had not been wiser than we were, we would all have been drowned at the wooden bridge."

I heard no more, as they went into the house, and John took me to the stable. Oh! what a good supper he gave me that night, a good bran mash and some crushed beans with my oats, and a thick bed of straw. I was glad of it, for I was tired.

13. The Devil's Trade Mark

ONE day when John and I had been out, and were returning gently on a long straight road, at some distance we saw a boy trying to leap a pony over a gate. The pony would not take the leap, and the boy cut him with the whip, but he only turned off on one side. Then the boy got off and gave him a hard thrashing, and hit him about the head; then he got up again and tried to make him leap the gate, kicking him all the time shamefully, but still the pony refused. When we were nearly at the sport, the pony put down his head and threw up his heels and sent the boy neatly over into a broad thorn hedge, and with the rein dangling from his head, he set off home at a full gallop. John laughed out loud. "Served him right," he said.

"Help!" cried the boy, as he struggled about among the thorns. "I say, come and help me out."

"I think you are in the right place," said John, "and maybe a little scratching will teach you not to leap a pony over a gate that is too high for him," and with that he rode off. "It may be," said he, "that young fellow is a liar as well as cruel; we'll just go home by Farmer Bushby's,

Beauty, and tell 'em." So we turned off to the right, and soon came within sight of the house. The farmer was hurrying out into the road, and his wife was standing at the gate, looking very frightened.

"Have you seen my boy?" said Mr. Bushby, as we came up. "He went out an hour ago on my black pony, and it has just come back without a rider."

"I should think, sir," said John, "he had better stay without a rider, unless he can be ridden properly."

"What do you mean?" said the farmer.

"Well, sir, I saw your son whipping, and kicking, and hitting that good little pony shamefully because he would not leap a gate that was too high for him. The pony behaved well, sir, and showed no temper; but at last he just threw up his heels, and tipped the young gentleman into the thorn hedge. He wanted me to help him out; but I hope you will excuse me, sir, I did not feel inclined to do so. There's no bones broken, sir, he'll only get a few scratches. I love horses, and hate to see them badly used. It is a bad plan to aggravate an animal until he uses his heels; the first time is not always the last."

During this time the mother began to cry, "Oh! my poor Bill, I must go and meet him, he must be hurt."

"You had better go into the house, wife," said the farmer. "Bill needs a lesson about this, and I must see that he gets it; this is not the first time that he has ill-used that pony, and I shall stop it. I am much obliged to you, Manly. Good evening."

So we went on, John chuckling all the way home. He told James about it, who laughed and said. "Serve him right. I knew that boy at school; he put on great airs because he was a farmer's son. He used to swagger about and bully the little boys. Of course, we elder ones would not have any of that nonsense, and let him know that in the school farmers' sons and working men's sons were all alike. I well remember one day, just before afternoon school, I found him catching flies and pulling off their wings. He did not see me, and I gave him a blow on the ears that laid him sprawling on the floor. Well, angry as I was, I was almost frightened, he roared and bellowed in such a style. The boys and the master rushed in from the playground, to see who was being murdered. Of course I told them what I had done, and why. Then I showed the master the poor flies, some crushed and some crawling about helpless, and I showed him the wings on the window sill. I never saw him so angry before; but as Bill was still howling and whining, like the coward that he was, he did not give him any more punishment of that kind, but set him up on a stool for the rest of the afternoon, and said that he should not go out to play for that week. Then he talked to all the boys very seriously about cruelty, and said how wicked it was to hurt the weak and the helpless. But what stuck in my mind was this: he said that cruelty was the devil's own trade mark, and if we saw any one who took pleasure in cruelty, we might know who he belonged to, for the devil was a murderer from the beginning, and a tormentor to the end. On the other hand, where we saw people who loved their friends, and were kind to man and beast, we might know that was God's mark, for 'God is Love'."

"Your master never taught you a truer thing," said John. "People may talk as much as they like about their religion, but if it does not teach them to be good and kind to men and beast, it is all a sham, and it won't stand when things come to be turned inside out and put down for what they are."

14. James Howard

ONE morning early in December, John had just led me into my box after my daily exercise, and James was coming in with some oats, when the master came into the stable.

"Good morning, John," said the master. "I want to know if you have any complaint to make of James?"

"Complaint, sir? No, sir."

"Is he industrious at his work and respectful to you?"

"Yes, sir, always."

"You never find he neglects his work when your back is turned?"

"Never, sir."

"Have you any reason to suspect that when he goes out with the horses, he hangs about talking to his acquaintances, or goes into houses where he has no business, leaving the horses outside?"

"No, sir, certainly not, and if anybody has been saying that about James, I don't believe it. A steadier, pleasanter. honester, smarter young fellow I never had in this stable. I can trust his word and I can trust his work; he is gentle and clever with the horses, and I would rather have them in his charge than in that of half the young fellows I know in laced hats and liveries, and whoever wants a character of James Howard," said John, with a decided jerk of his head, "let them come to John Manly."

The master stood all this time grave and attentive, but as John finished his speech, a broad smile spread over his face, and looking kindly across at James, who all this time had stood still at the door, he said, "James, my lad, set down the oats and come here. I am very glad to find that John's opinion of your character agrees so exactly with my own. John is a cautious man," he added, "and it is not always easy to get his opinion about people, so I thought if I beat the bush on this side, the birds would fly out, and I should learn what I wanted to know quickly; we will come to the point. My brother-in-law, Sir Clifford Williams, of Clifford Hall, wants me to find him a trustworthy young groom, about twenty or twenty-one, who knows his business. His old coachman, who has lived with him twenty years, is getting feeble, and he wants a man to work with him who would be able to step into his place when the old man is pensioned off. He would have eighteen shillings a week at first, a stable suit, a driving suit, a bedroom over the coachhouse, and a boy under him. Sir Clifford is a good master, and if you could get the place, it would be a good start for you. I don't want to part with you, and if you left us I know

John would lose his right hand."

"That I would, sir," said John, "but I would not stand in his way for the world."

"How old are you, James?" said master.

"Nineteen next May, sir."

"That's young; what do you think, John?"

"Well, sir, it is young: but he is as steady as a man, and is as strong, and well grown, and though he has not had much experience in driving, he has a light firm hand, and a quick eye, and he is very careful, and I am quite sure no horse of his will be ruined for want of care."

"Your word will go the furthest, John," said the master, "for Sir Clifford says, 'If I could find a man trained by your John, I should like him better than any other.' So think it over, James, lad, talk to your mother at dinnertime, and then let me know what you wish."

In a few days after this conversation, it was fully settled that James should go to Clifford Hall in five or six weeks, and in the meantime he was to get all the practice in driving that he could. I never knew the carriage to go out so often before. Ginger and I were put into double harness and James drove us. At first, John rode with him on the box, but soon James drove alone.

Then it was wonderful what a number of places the master would go to in the city on Saturday, and what queer streets we were driven through. He was sure to go to the railway station just as the train was coming in, and cabs and carriages, carts and omnibuses were all trying to get over the bridge together. That bridge needed good horses and good drivers when the railway bell was ringing, for it was narrow, and there was a very sharp turn up to the station, where people needed to look carefully and keep their wits about them.

15. The Old Ostler

AFTER this my master and mistress decided to visit some friends who lived about forty-six miles from our home, and James was to drive them. The first day we went thirty-two miles. There were some long heavy hills, but James drove so carefully and thoughtfully that we were not at all harassed. He never forgot to put on the brake as we went downhill, nor to take it off at the right place. He kept our feet on the smoothest part of the road, and if the uphill was very long, he set the carriage wheels a little across the road, so as not to run back, and gave us a breathing space. All these little things help a horse very much, particularly if he gets kind words as well.

We stopped once or twice on the road, and at sunset we reached the town where we were to spend the night. We stopped at the principal hotel, which was in the market place. We drove under an archway into a long yard, at the further end of which were the stables and coach-houses. Two ostlers came to take us out. The head ostler was a pleasant, active little man, with a crooked leg, and a yellow striped waistcoat. I never saw a man unbuckle harness as quickly as he did, and with a pat and a good word he led me to a long stable, with six or eight stalls in it, and two or three horses. The other man brought Ginger. James stood by while we were rubbed down and cleaned.

I never was cleaned so lightly and quickly as by that little old man. When he had done, James stepped up and felt me over, as if he thought I could not be thoroughly done, but he found my coat as clean and smooth as silk.

"Well," he said, "I thought I was pretty quick, and our

John quicker still, but you beat all I ever saw for being quick and thorough at the same time."

"Practice makes perfect," said the crooked little ostler, "and I've had forty years of it; and as to being quick, why, bless you! that is only a matter of habit; if you get into the habit of being quick, it is just as easy as being slow – easier, I should say. In fact, it don't agree with my health to be dawdling about over a job twice as long as it need take. You see, I have been about horses ever since I was twelve years old, in hunting stables, and racing stables; and being small, ye see, I was jockey for several years. But at Goodwood, ye see, my poor Larkspur got a fall, and I broke my knee, and so of course I was of no more use there. But I could not live without horses, of course I couldn't, so I took to the hotels. I can tell ye it is a downright pleasure to handle an animal like this, well-bred, well-mannered, well-cared for. Give me the handling of a horse for twenty minutes, and I'll tell you what sort of a groom he has had. Look at this one, pleasant, quiet, turns about just as you want him, holds up his feet to be cleaned out, or anything else you please. Then you'll find another, fidgety, fretty, won't move the right way, or starts across the stall, tosses up his head as soon as you come near him, lays his ears, and seems afraid of you, or else lunges about at you with his heels! Poor things! I know what sort of treatment they have had. Horses are like children; train 'em up in the way they should go, as the good book says, and when they are old they will not depart from it – if they have a chance, that is."

"I like to hear you talk," said James. "That's the way we lay it down at home, at our master's."

"Who is your master, young man? I should judge he is

a good one, from what I see."

"He is Squire Gordon, of Birtwick Park, the other side of the Beacon hills," said James.

"Ah! I have heard tell of him; fine judge of horses, ain't he? the best rider in the country?"

"I believe he is," said James, "but he rides very little now, since the poor young master was killed."

"Ah! poor gentleman. I read all about it in the paper at the time; a fine horse killed too, wasn't there?"

"Yes," said James, "he was a splendid creature, brother to this one, and just like him."

"Pity! pity!" said the old man. "'Twas a bad place to leap, if I remember; a thin fence at top, a steep bank down to the stream, wasn't it? no chance for a horse to see where he is going. There are some leaps that only a very knowing old huntsman has any right to take; a man's life and a horse's life are worth more than a fox's tail, at least I should say they ought to be."

16. The Fire

LATER on in the evening, a stranger's horse was brought in by the second ostler, and while he was cleaning him, a young man with a pipe in his mouth lounged in to talk.

"I say, Towler," said the ostler, "just run up the ladder into the loft and put some hay down into this horse's rack, will you? But lay down your pipe first."

Towler went up through the trap door; and I heard him step across the floor overhead and put down the hay. James came in to look at us the last thing, and then the door was locked.

I cannot say what time in the night it was, but I woke up feeling very uncomfortable. The air seemed all thick and choking. I heard Ginger coughing and one of the horses moved about restlessly. It was quite dark, and I could see nothing, but the stable was very full of smoke, and I could hardly breathe.

The trap door had been left open, and I thought that was the place it came through. I listened and heard a soft rushing sort of noise, and a low crackling and snapping. I did not know what it was, but there was something in the sound so strange that it made me tremble all over. The other horses were now all awake; some were pulling at their halters, others were stamping.

At last I heard steps outside, and the ostler who had put up the stranger's horse burst into the stable with a lantern, and began to untie the horses, and try to lead them out. He seemed in such a hurry and so frightened that he frightened me still more. The first horse would not go with him. He tried the second and third; they too would not stir. He came to me next and tried to drag me out of the stall by force. He tried us all by turns and then left the stable.

No doubt we were very foolish, but danger seemed to be all around and there was nobody we knew to trust in. The fresh air that had come in through the open door made it easier to breathe, but the rushing sound overhead grew louder, and as I looked upward, I saw a red light flickering on the wall. Then I heard a cry of "Fire" outside, and the old ostler quietly and quickly came in. He got one horse out, and went to another, but the flames were playing around the trap door, and the roaring overhead was dreadful.

The next thing I heard was James's voice, quiet and cheery, as it always was.

"Come, my beauties, it is time for us to be off, so wake up and come along." I stood nearest the door, so he came to me first, patting me as he came in.

"Come, Beauty, on with your bridle, my boy, we'll soon be out of this smother." It was on in no time. Then he took the scarf off his neck, and tied it lightly over my eyes, and patting and coaxing he led me out of the stable. Safe in the yard, he slipped the scarf off my eyes, and shouted, "Here, somebody! take this horse while I go back for the other."

A man stepped forward and took me, and James darted back into the stable. I set up a shrill whinny as I saw him go. Ginger told me afterwards that whinny was the best thing I could have done for her, for had she not heard me outside, she would never have had the courage to come out.

There was much confusion in the yard; the horses being got out of other stables, and the carriages and gigs being pulled out of houses and sheds. On the other side

90

of the yard, windows were thrown up, and people were shouting, but I kept my eye fixed on the stable door, where the smoke poured out thicker than ever, and I could see flashes of red light. Presently I heard above all the stir and din loud clear voice, which I knew was master's:

"James Howard! James Howard! are you there?" There was no answer, but I heard a crash of something falling in the stable, and the next moment I gave a loud joyful neigh, for I saw James coming through the smoke leading Ginger with him.

"My brave lad!" said master, laying his hand on his shoulder, "are you hurt?"

James shook his head, for he could not yet speak.

"Aye," said the man who held me, "he is a brave lad, and no mistake."

"And now," said master, "we'll get out of this place as quickly as we can," and we were moving towards the entry, when from the market place there came a sound of galloping feet and loud rumbling wheels.

"The fire engine! the fire engine!" shouted two or three voices, and clattering and thundering over the stones two horses dashed into the yard with the heavy engine behind them. The firemen leaped to the ground. There was no need to ask where the fire was – it was torching up in a great blaze from the roof.

We got out as fast as we could into the broad quiet market place; the stars were shining, and, except for the noise behind us, all was still. Master led the way to a large hotel on the other side, and as soon as the ostler came, he said, "James, I must now hurry to your mistress; I trust the horses entirely to you, order whatever you think is needed," and with that he was gone. The master did not run, but I never saw mortal man walk as fast as he did that night.

There was a dreadful sound before we got into our stalls – the shrieks of those poor horses that were left burning to death in the stable.

The next morning the master came to see how we were and to speak to James. I did not hear much, for the ostler was rubbing me down, but I could see that James looked very happy, and I thought the master was proud of him. Our mistress had been so much alarmed in the night that the journey was put off until the afternoon, so James had the morning free, and went first to the inn to see about our harness and the carriage, and then to hear more about the fire. When he came back, we heard him tell the ostler about it. At first no one could guess how the fire had been caused, but at last a man said he saw Dick Towler go into the stable with a pipe in his mouth, and come out without one. Then the under ostler said he had asked Dick to go up the ladder to put down some hay, but told him to lay down his pipe first. Dick denied taking the pipe with him, but no one believed him. I remember John Manly's rule, never to allow a pipe in the stable, and thought it ought to be the rule everywhere.

James said the roof and floor had all fallen in, and that only the black walls were standing. The two poor horses that could not be got out were buried under the burned rafters and tiles.

17. John Manly's Talk

A LITTLE after sunset we reached the house of my master's friend. We were taken into a clean snug stable; there was a kind coachman who seemed to think a good deal of James when he heard about the fire.

"There is one thing quite clear, young man," he said, "your horses know who they can trust. It is one of the hardest things in the world to get horses out of a stable when there is either fire or flood. I don't know why they won't come out, but they won't – not one in twenty."

We stopped two or three days at this place and then returned home. All went well on the journey; we were glad to be in our own stable again, and John was equally glad to see us.

Before he and James left us for the night, James said, "I wonder who is coming in my place."

"Little Joe Green at the Lodge," said John.

"Joe! why, he's a child!"

"He is fourteen and a half," said John.

"But he is such a little chap."

"Yes, but he is quick, and willing, and kindhearted too, and then he wishes very much to come, and his father would like it. And I know the master would like to give him the chance. He said, if I thought he would not do, he would look out for a bigger boy, but I said I was quite agreeable to try him for six weeks."

"Six weeks!" said James, "why, it will be six months before he can be of much use! It will make you a lot of work, John."

"Well," said John with a laugh, "I never was afraid of work yet."

"You are a very good man," said James, "I wish I may ever be like you."

"I was just as old as Joseph," said John, "when my father and mother died of the fever, within ten days of each other, and left me and my crippled sister Nelly alone in the world. I was a farmer's boy, not earning enough to keep myself, much less both of us, and she would have gone to the poorhouse, but for our mistress (Nelly calls her her angel, and she's right). She hired a room for her, and gave her knitting and needlework, when she was able to do it, and when she was ill, she sent her dinners and many nice comfortable things, and was like a mother to her. The master took me into the stable under old Norman, the coachman that was then. I had my food at the house, and my bed in the loft, and a suit of clothes and three shillings a week, so that I could help Nelly. Then there was Norman; he might have refused to be troubled at his age with a raw boy, but he took no end of pains with me. When he died some years after, I stepped into his place, and now of course I have top wages and can save for a rainy day, and Nelly is as happy as a bird. So you see, James, I am not the man who would turn up his nose at a little boy. No! no! I shall miss you very much, James, but we shall pull through, and there's nothing like doing a kindness when 'tis put in your way, and I am glad I can do it."

"Then," said James, "you don't hold with that saying, 'Everybody look after himself, and take care of number one.'"

"No, indeed," said John, "where should I and Nelly have been, if master and mistress and old Norman had only taken care of number one? Why – she in the poorhouse and I hoeing turnips! Where would Black Beauty and Ginger have been if you had only thought of number one? Why, roasted to death! No, Jim, no! that is a selfish, heathenish saying, and any man who thinks he has nothing to do but take care of number one, why, it's a pity that he wasn't drowned like a puppy or a kitten, before he got his eyes open. That's what I think," said John, with a very decided jerk of his head.

James laughed at this, but there was a thickness in his voice when he said, "You have been my best friend except my mother; I hope you won't forget me."

"No, lad, no!" said John, "and if ever I can do you a good turn, I hope you won't forget me."

The next day Joe came to the stables to learn all he could before James left. He learned to sweep the stable, to bring in the straw and hay; he began to clean the harness, and helped to wash the carriage. As he was too short to groom Ginger and me, James taught him upon Merrylegs. He was a nice bright little fellow, and always came whistling to his work.

Merrylegs was a good deal put out at being "mauled about," as he said, "by a boy who knew nothing," but towards the end of the second week he told me confidentially that he thought the boy would turn out well.

At last the day came when James had to leave us. Cheerful as he always was, he looked quite downhearted that morning.

"You see," he said to John, "I am leaving a great deal behind – my mother and Betsy, and you, and a good master and mistress, and then the horses, and my old Merrylegs. At the new place, there will not be a soul I know. If it were not that I shall get a higher place, and be able to help my mother better, I don't think I would have made up my mind to it; it is a real hardship, John."

"Aye, James, lad, so it is. But I should not think much of you, if you could leave your home for the first time and not feel it. Cheer up, you'll make friends there, and if you get on well – as I am sure you will, it will be a fine thing for your mother, and she will be proud that you have made such a good start."

Everyone was sorry to lose James; as for Merrylegs, he pined after him for several days, and went quite off his appetite. So John took him out several mornings with a leading rein when he exercised me, and trotting and galloping by my side soon cheered him up.

Joe's father would often come in and give a little help, as he understood the work, and Joe took a great deal of pains to learn, and John was quite encouraged about him.

18. Going for the Doctor

ONE night, a few days after James had left, I was fast asleep in my straw, when I was suddenly awakened by the stable bell. I heard the door of John's house open, and his feet running up to the Hall. He was back again in no time. He unlocked the stable door, and came in, calling out, "Wake up, Beauty, you must go well now, if ever you did," and almost before I could think, he had got the saddle on my back and the bridle on my head and took me at a quick trot up to the Hall door. The Squire stood there with a lamp in his hand.

"Now, John," he said, "ride for your mistress's life! There is not a moment to lose! Give this note to Doctor White, and be back as soon as you can."

John said, "Yes, sir," and was on my back in a minute. The gardener who lived at the lodge had heard the bell ring, and was ready with the gate open, and away we went through the Park and through the village and down the hill until we came to the tollgate. John called very loud and thumped upon the door: the man was soon out and flung open the gate.

"Now," said John, "keep the gate open for the Doctor. Here's the money," and off we went again.

There was before us a long piece of level road by the river side. John said to me, "Now Beauty, do your best," and so I did. I needed no whip nor spur, and for two miles I galloped as fast as I could lay my feet to the ground; I don't believe that my old grandfather who won the race at Newmarket could have gone faster. When we came to the bridge, John pulled me up a little and patted my neck. "Well done, Beauty! good old fellow," he said.

He would have let me go slower, but my spirit was up, and I was off again as fast as before. The air was frosty and the moon was bright. We came through a village, then through a dark wood, then uphill, then downhill, until after an eight mile run we came to the town, through the streets and into the market place. It was all quite still except the clatter of my feet on the stones. The church clock struck three as we drew up at Doctor White's door.

John rang the ball twice, and then knocked at the door like thunder. A window was thrown up, and Doctor White, in his nightcap, put his head out and said, "What do you want?"

"Mrs. Gordon is very ill, sir. Master wants you to go at once, he thinks she will die if you cannot get there – here is a note."

"Wait," he said, "I will come."

He shut the window, and was soon at the door.

"The worst of it is," he said, "that my horse has been out all day and is quite worn out; my son has just been sent for, and he has taken the other. What is to be done? Can I have your horse?"

"He has come at a gallop nearly all the way, sir, and I meant to give him a rest here; but I think my master would not be against it if you think, sir."

"All right," he said. "I will soon be ready."

John stood by me and stroked my neck; I was very hot. The Doctor came out with his riding whip.

"You need not take that, sir," said John. "Black Beauty will go until he drops. Take care of him, sir, if you can. I should not like any harm to come to him."

"No! no! John," said the Doctor, "I hope not," and in a minute we had left John far behind.

I will not tell about our way back; the Doctor was a heavier man than John, and not so good a rider. However, I did my very best. The man at the tollgate had it open. When we came to the hill, the Doctor drew me up. "Now my good fellow," he said, "take some breath." I was glad he did, for I was nearly spent, but that breathing space helped me on, and soon we were in the Park. My master was at the Hall door, for he had heard us coming. He spoke not a word; the Doctor went into the house with him and Joe led me to the stable.

I was glad to get home, my legs shook under me, and I could only stand and pant. I had not a dry hair on my body, the water ran down my legs, and I steamed all over. Poor Joe! as yet he knew very little, and his father, who would have helped him was not there but I am sure he did his very best. He rubbed my legs and my chest, but he did not put my warm cloth on me – he thought I was so hot I should not like it. Then he gave me a pail full of water to drink; it was cold and I drank it all; then he gave me some hay and some corn, and thinking he had done right, he went away. Soon I began to shake and tremble, and turned deadly cold, my legs ached, my loins ached, and my chest ached, and I felt sore all over. Oh! how I wished for my warm thick cloth as I stood and trembled. I wanted John, but he had eight miles to walk, so I lay down in my straw and tried to go to sleep. After a long while I heard John at the door. I gave a low moan, for I was in great pain.

He was at my side in a moment, stooping down by me. I could not tell him how I felt, but he seemed to know it all; he covered me up with some warm cloths, and then ran to the house for some hot water. He made me some warm gruel which I drank, and then I think I went to sleep.

John seemed to be very much put out. I heard him say to himself, over and over again, "Stupid boy! stupid boy! no cloth put on, and I dare say the water was cold too! Boys are no good!" but Joe was a good boy after all.

I was now very ill; my lungs were badly inflamed and I could not draw my breath without pain. John nursed me night and day, and would get up two or three times in the night to come to me. My master, too, often came to see me.

"My poor Beauty," he said one day, "you saved her life." It seems the Doctor had said if we had been a little longer it would have been too late. John told my master he never saw a horse go so fast in his life; it seemed as if the horse knew what was the matter. Of course I did – at least I knew that we must go at top speed, and that it was for the sake of the mistress.

19. Only Ignorance

I DO not know how long I was ill. The horse doctor came every day. One day he bled me; John held a pail for the blood. I felt very faint after it, and thought I would die, and I believe they all thought so too.

Ginger and Merrylegs had been moved into the other stable, so that I might be quiet, for the fever made me very quick of hearing; any little noise seemed quite loud, and I could tell every one's footstep going to and from the house. One night John had to give me some medicine. Tom Green came in to help him. After I had taken it and John had made me as comfortable as he could, he said he would stay half an hour to see how the medicine settled. Tom said he would stay with him, so they went and sat down on a bench that had been brought into Merryleg's stall, and put down the lantern at their feet, that I might not be disturbed by the light.

For a while both men sat silent, and then Tom Green said in a low voice:

"I wish, John, you'd say a kind word to Joe; the boy is quite brokenhearted. He says he knows it was all his fault, though he is sure he did the best he knew, and he says, if Beauty dies, no one will ever speak to him again. It goes to my heart to hear him. I think you might give him just a word; he is not a bad boy."

After a short pause, John said slowly, "You must not be too hard upon me, Tom. I know he meant no harm, I never said he did; I know he is not a bad boy, but you see; that horse is the pride of my heart, to say nothing of his being such a pet of the master and mistress; and to think that his life may be flung away in this manner, is

more than I can bear. But if you think I am hard on the
boy, I will try to give him a good word tomorrow – that
is, I mean, if Beauty is better."

"Well, John! thank you. I knew you did not wish to be
too hard, and I am glad you see it was only ignorance."

John's voice almost startled me as he answered, "*Only* ignorance! how can you talk about *only* ignorance? Don't you know that it is the worst thing in the world, next to wickedness? – and which does the most mischief, heaven only knows. If people can say, 'Oh! I did not know, I did not mean any harm,' they think it is all right. I suppose Martha Mulwash did not mean to kill that baby, when she dosed it with soothing syrups; but she did kill it, and was tried for manslaughter."

"And served her right, too," said Tom, "A woman should not undertake to nurse a baby without knowing what to give it."

"Bill Starkey," continued John, "did not mean to terrify his brother when he dressed up like a ghost, and ran after him in the moonlight. But he did – and that bright, handsome little fellow, who might have been the pride of any mother's heart, is just no better than an idiot, and never will be, if he lives to be eighty years old. You were a good deal put out yourself, Tom, two weeks ago, when those young ladies left your hothouse door open, with an east wind blowing right in; you said it killed a good many of your plants."

"A good many!" said Tom. "There was not one of the tender cuttings that was not nipped off. I shall have to strike all over again. And the worst of it is, that I don't know where to go to get fresh ones. I was nearly mad when I came in and saw what was done."

"And yet," said John, "I am sure the young ladies did not mean it; it was only ignorance!"

I heard no more of this conversation, for the medicine did well and sent me to sleep, and in the morning I felt much better, but I often thought of John's words when I came to know more of the world.

20. Joe Green

JOE GREEN learned very quickly, and John began to trust him in many things. He was so small that he was seldom allowed to exercise either Ginger or me; but it so happened one morning that John was out with Justice in the luggage cart, and the master wanted a note taken immediately to a gentleman's house, about three miles away, and sent his orders for Joe to saddle me and take it; adding the caution that he was to ride carefully.

On our way back we passed Mr. Clay's brickyard. Here we saw a cart heavily laden with bricks. The wheels had stuck fast in the mud and the carter was shouting and whipping the two horses unmercifully. Joe pulled up. It was a sad sight. There were the two horses straining with all their might to drag the cart out, but they could not move it. The sweat streamed from their legs and flanks, their sides heaved, and every muscle was strained, the man, fiercely pulling at the head of the leading horse, swore and lashed most brutally.

"Hold hard!" said Joe, "don't go on whipping the horses like that. The wheels are so stuck that they cannot move the cart." The man took no notice, but went on lashing.

"Stop, stop!" said Joe. "I'll help you to lighten the cart – they can't move it now."

"Mind your own business, you impudent young rascal and I'll mind mine." The man was in a towering passion and the worse for drink, and laid on the whip again. Joe turned my head, and the next moment we were going at full gallop towards Mr. Clay's house. I cannot say if John would have approved of our pace, but Joe and I were both of one mind, and so angry that we could not have gone slower.

Joe knocked at the door and shouted, "Hullo! is Mr. Clay at home?" The door was opened, and Mr. Clay himself came out.

"Hullo young man! you seem in a hurry. Any orders from the squire this morning?"

"No, Mr. Clay, but there's a fellow in your brickyard whipping two horses to death. I told him to stop and he wouldn't; so I have come to tell you." Joe's voice shook with excitement.

"Thank ye, my lad," said the man. "Will you give evidence of what you saw if I should bring the fellow up before a magistrate?"

"That I will," said Joe, "and glad to." The man was gone, and we were on our way home at a smart trot.

"Why, what's the matter with you, Joe? You look

angry all over," said John, as the boy flung himself from the saddle.

"I am angry all over, I can tell you," said the boy. Then he told all that had happened. Joe was usually such a quiet, gentle little fellow that it was wonderful to see him so aroused.

"You did right, my boy, whether the fellow gets a summons or not. Many folk would have ridden by and said 'twas not their business to interfere. Now, I say that with cruelty and oppression it is everybody's business to interfere when they see it. You did right, my boy."

Joe was proud that John approved of him, and he cleaned out my feet and rubbed me down with a firmer hand than usual.

They were just going home to dinner when the footman came down to the stable to say that Joe was wanted in master's study; there was a man brought up for ill-using horses, and Joe's evidence was wanted. Our master being one of the county magistrates, cases were often brought to him to settle, or say what should be done.

When Joe next came into the stable I saw he was in high spirits. He gave me a good-natured slap and said, "We won't see such things done, will we, old fellow?" We heard afterwards that he had given his evidence so clearly, and the horses were in such an exhausted state, bearing marks of such brutal usage, that the carter was committed to take his trial, and might possibly be sentenced to two or three months in prison.

It was wonderful what a change had come over Joe. John said he had grown an inch taller in that week. He was just as kind and gentle as before, but there was more purpose and determination in all that he did – as if he had jumped at once from a boy into a man.

21. The Parting

I HAD now lived in this happy place three years, but sad changes were about to come over us.

We already knew that our mistress was ill. Now we heard that she must leave her home at once and go to a warm country for two or three years. The news fell upon the household like the tolling of a death-bell. The master at once began to make arrangements for breaking up his home and leaving England.

The first of the party who went were Miss Jessie and Flora with their governess. They came to bid us good-bye. They hugged poor Merrylegs like the old friend he was. Then we heard what had been arranged for us. Master had sold Ginger and me to his old friend, the Earl of W—, for he thought we would have a good place there. Merrylegs he had given to the Vicar, who was wanting a pony for Mrs. Blomefield, but it was on the condition that he should never be sold.

Joe was engaged to take care of him, and to help in the house, so I thought that Merrylegs was well off. John had the offer of several good places, but he said he would wait a little and look around.

The evening before they left, the master came into the stable for the last time. I knew by his voice that he was very unhappy.

"Have you decided what to do, John?" he said. 'I find you have not accepted any of those offers."

"No, sir, I have made up my mind that if I could get a situation with some good colt-breaker and horsetrainer, it would be the right thing for me. Many young animals are frightened and spoiled by wrong treatment which need not be, if the right man took them in hand. I always get on well with horses, and if I could help some of them to a fair start. I would feel I was doing some good. What do you think of it, sir?"

"I don't know a man anywhere," said the master, "that I should think so suitable for it. You understand horses, and somehow they understand you, and in time you might set up for yourself; I think you could not do better. If in any way I can help you, write to me; I shall speak to my agent in London."

Master gave John the name and address, and then he thanked him for his long and faithful service, but that was too much for John. "Pray don't, sir, I can't bear it; you and my dear mistress have done so much for me that I could never repay it. We shall never forget you, sir, and please God we may some day see mistress back again and like herself." Master gave John his hand, but he did not speak, and they both left the stable.

The last sad day had come. The footman and the heavy luggage had gone off the day before, and there were only master and mistress and her maid. Ginger and I brought the carriage up to the Hall door for the last time. Master came down the steps carrying the mistress in his arms; he placed her carefully in the carriage, while the house servants stood around crying.

"Good-bye again," he said, "we will not forget any of you," and he got in. "Drive on, John."

Joe jumped up, and we trotted slowly through the Park, and through the village, where the people were standing at their doors to have a last look.

When we reached the railway station, mistress walked from the carriage to the waiting room. I heard her sweet voice say, "Good-bye, John, God bless you." I felt the rein twitch, but John made no answer; perhaps he could not speak. As soon as Joe had taken the things out of the carriage, John called him to stand by the horses, while he went on the platform. Poor Joe! he stood close up to our heads to hide his tears. Very soon the train came puffing up into the station. Two or three minutes later the doors were slammed to; the guard whistled and the train glided away, leaving behind it only clouds of white smoke and some very heavy hearts.

When it was quite out of sight, John came back:

"We shall never see her again," he said – "never." He took the reins, mounted the box, and with Joe drove slowly home; but it was not our home now.

22. Earlshall

THE next morning after breakfast Joe took Merrylegs to the vicarage. He came first and said good-bye to us, and Merrylegs neighed to us from the yard. Then John put the saddle on Ginger and the leading rein on me, and rode us across country to Earlshall Park, where the Earl of W— lived. There was a very fine house and a great deal of stabling. We went into the yard through a stone gateway, and John asked for Mr. York. It was some time before he came. He was a fine-looking, middle-aged man, and his voice said at once that he expected to be obeyed. He was very friendly and polite to John, and he called a groom to take us to our boxes, and invited John to take some refreshment.

We were taken to a light airy stable, and placed in adjoining boxes where we were rubbed down and fed. In about half an hour John and Mr. York, who was to be our new coachman, came in to see us.

"Now, Mr. Manly," he said, after carefully looking at us both, "do these horses have any particular habits that you would like to mention?"

"Well," said John, "I don't believe there is a better pair of horses in the country, and right grieved I am to part with them, but they are not alike. The black one has the most perfect temper I ever knew; I suppose he has never known a hard word or a blow since he was foaled. But the chestnut must have had bad treatment – we heard as much from the dealer. She came to us snappish and suspicious, but by degrees we cured her. Now I never see the smallest sign of temper, and if she is well treated there is not a better, more willing animal than she is. But she is naturally more irritable than the black horse. Flies tease her more; anything wrong in the harness frets her more; and if she were ill-used or unfairly treated, she would not be unlikely to give tit for tat."

"Of course," said York, "I quite understand, but you know it is not easy in stables like these to have all the grooms just what they should be."

They were going out of the stable when John said, "I had better mention that we have never used the 'bearing rein' with either of them. The black horse never had one on, and the dealer said it was the gag-bit that spoiled the other's temper."

"Well," said York, "if they come here they must wear the bearing rein. I prefer a loose rein myself, and his lordship is always very reasonable about horses – but my lady – that's another thing, she insists on style; and if her carriage horses are not reined up tight, she won't look at them. I don't like the gag-bit, but it must be tight up when my lady rides!"

"I am sorry for it, very sorry," said John; "but I must go now, or I shall lose the train."

He came around to each of us to pat and speak to us for the last time; his voice sounded very sad. I held my face close to him, and then he was gone, and I have never seen him since.

The next day Lord W— came to look at us. He seemed pleased with our appearance.

"I have great confidence in these horses," he said, "from my friend Mr. Gordon's report of them. Of course they do not match in colour, but my idea is that they will do very well for the carriage while we are in the country. Before we go to London I must try to match the black horse; I believe he is perfect for riding."

York then told him what John had said about us.

"Well," said he, "you must keep an eye to the mare, and put the bearing rein easy; I dare say they will do very well if they come to it gradually. I'll mention it to her ladyship."

In the afternoon we were harnessed and put in the carriage, and at three we were led around to the front of the house. It was all very grand, and much larger than the old house at Birtwick, but not half so pleasant, if a horse may have an opinion. Two footmen were standing ready, dressed in livery, with scarlet breeches and white stockings. Presently we heard the rustling sound of silk as my lady came down the stone steps. She was a tall, proud-looking woman, and did not seem pleased about something, but she said nothing, and got into the carriage. This was the first time I had worn a bearing rein, and I must say, though it certainly was a nuisance not to be able to get my head down now and then, it did not pull my head higher than I was accustomed to carry it. I felt anxious about Ginger, but she seemed to be quiet and content.

The next day at three o'clock we were again at the door, and the footmen as before. We heard the silk dress rustle, and the lady came down the steps, and in an imperious voice she said, "York, you must put those horses' heads higher; they are not fit to be seen."

York said very respectfully, "I beg your pardon, my lady, but these horses have not been reined up for three years, and my lord said it would be safer to bring them to it by degrees. But if your ladyship pleases, I can take them up a little more."

"Do so," she said.

York came around to our heads and shortened the rein himself, one hole, I think; every little makes a difference, be it for better or worse. That day we had a steep hill to go up. Then I began to understand what I had heard. Of course I wanted to put my head forward and take the carriage up with a will, as we had always done, but no, I had to pull with my head up now, and that took all the spirit out of me, and the strain came on my back and legs. When we came in, Ginger said, "Now you see what it is like. If it does not get much worse than this, I shall say nothing about it, for we are very well treated here. But if they strain me up tight, why, let 'em look out! I can't bear it, and I won't."

Day by day, hole by hole our bearing reins were shortened, and instead of looking forward with pleasure to having my harness put on as I used to do, I began to dread it. Ginger too seemed restless, though she said very little. At last I thought the worst was over; for several days there was no more shortening, and I determined to make the best of it and do my duty, though it was now a constant burden instead of a pleasure. But the worst was to come.

23. A Strike for Liberty

ONE day my lady came down later than usual, and the silk rustled more than ever.

"Drive to the Duchess of B—'s," she said, "Are you never going to get those horses' heads up, York? Raise them at once, and let us have no more of this nonsense."

York came to me first, while the groom stood at Ginger's head. He drew my head back and fixed the rein so tight that it was almost intolerable. Then he went to Ginger, who was impatiently jerking her head up and down against the bit, as was her way now. She knew what was coming, and the moment York took the rein off the harness ring in order to shorten it, she seized her opportunity, and reared up so suddenly that York had his nose roughly hit and the groom was nearly thrown off his legs. At once they both flew to her head, but she went on plunging, rearing, and kicking in a most desperate manner. At last she kicked right over the carriage pole and fell down, giving me a severe blow on my near quarter. York promptly sat down flat on her head to prevent her struggling, at the same time calling out, "Unbuckle the black horse! run for the winch and unscrew the carriage pole. Cut the trace here, somebody, if you can't unhitch it." One of the footmen ran for the winch, and another brought a knife from the house. The groom soon set me free from Ginger and the carriage, and led me to my box.

He just turned me in as I was and ran back to York. I was much excited by what had happened, and if I had ever kicked or reared, I am sure I should have done it then; but I never had, and there I stood angry, sore in my leg, my head still strained up to the harness ring on the saddle, I was very miserable, and felt much inclined to kick the first person who came near me.

Before long, however, Ginger was led in, a good deal knocked about and bruised. York came with her and gave his orders, and then came to look at me. He at once let down my head.

"Confound these bearing reins!" he said to himself; "I thought we should have some mischief soon – the master will be sorely vexed; but there – if a woman's husband can't rule her, of course a servant can't."

He felt me all over, and soon found the place above my hock where I had been kicked. It was swelled and painful; he ordered it to be sponged with hot water, and then some lotion was put on.

Lord W— was much put out when he learned what had happened. He blamed York for giving way to his mistress, and York replied that in future he would much prefer to receive his orders only from his lordship. But I think nothing came of it, for things went on the same as before. I thought York might have stood up better for his horses, but perhaps I am no judge.

Ginger was never put into the carriage again but when she had recovered, one of Lord W—'s younger sons said he should like to have her as a hunter. As for me, I was obliged still to go in the carriage, and had a fresh partner called Max. He had always been used to the tight rein. I asked him how it was he bore it.

"Well," he said, "I bear it because I must, but it is

shortening my life, and it will shorten yours too, if you have to stick to it."

"Do you think," I said, "that our masters know how bad it is for us?"

"I can't say," he replied, "but the dealers and the horse doctors know it very well. I was at a dealer's once, who was training me and another horse to go as a pair; he was getting our heads up, as he said, a little higher and a little higher every day. A gentleman who was there asked him why he did so. 'Because,' said he, 'people won't buy them unless we do. Of course it is very bad for the horses, but then it is good for trade. The horses soon wear out and they come for another pair.'"

What I suffered with that rein for four long months it would be hard to describe, but I am quite sure that, had it lasted much longer, either my health or my temper would have given way. Before that, I never knew what it was to foam at the mouth, but now the action of the sharp bit on my tongue and jaw, and the constrained position of my head and throat always caused me to froth at the mouth more or less. Some people think it very fine to see this, and say, "What fine, spirited creatures!" But foaming at the mouth is just as unnatural for horses as for men. Besides this, there was a pressure on my windpipe, which often made my breathing very uncomfortable. When I returned from my work, my neck and chest were strained and painful, my mouth and tongue tender, and I felt worn and depressed.

In my old home I always knew that John and my master were my friends; but here, although in many ways I was well treated, I had no friend. York knew how that rein harassed me, but I suppose he took it as a matter of course; at any rate, nothing was done to relieve me.

24. The Lady Anne

EARLY in the spring, Lord W— and part of his family went up to London, and took York with them. Ginger and I and some other horses were left at home, and Reuben Smith was left in charge.

Lady Harriet, who remained at the Hall, was an invalid, and never went out in the carriage, and Lady Anne preferred riding on horseback. She was a perfect horsewoman, and as gay and gentle as she was beautiful. She chose me for her horse, and named me "Black Auster". I very much enjoyed these rides in the clear cold air, sometimes with Ginger, sometimes with Lizzie. This Lizzie was a bright bay mare, popular with the gentlemen, on account of her fine action and lively spirit; but Ginger, who knew her better than I did, told me she was rather nervous. There was a Colonel Blantyre staying at the Hall. He always rode Lizzie, and praised her so much that one day Lady Anne ordered the sidesaddle to be put on her, and the other saddle on me. When we came to the door, the gentleman seemed very uneasy.

"How is this?" he said. "Are you tired of your good Black Auster?"

"Oh! no, not at all," she replied, "but I am going to let you ride him for once, and I will try your charming Lizzie. You must confess that in size and appearance she is far more like a lady's horse than is Black Auster."

"Do let me advise you not to mount her," he said. "She is a charming creature, but she is too nervous for a lady."

"My dear cousin," said Lady Anne, laughing, "pray do not trouble your good careful head about me. I have been a horsewoman ever since I was a baby, and I have followed the hounds a great many times, and I intend to try this Lizzie that you gentlemen are all so fond of, so please help me to mount."

There was no more to be said. He placed her carefully on the saddle and then mounted me. Just as we were moving off, a footman came out with a slip of paper and message from Lady Harriet – "Would they take this note for her to Doctor Ashley and bring the answer?"

The Doctor's house was about a mile off. There was a short drive up to the house. Blantyre got off at the gate, and was going to open it for Lady Anne, but she said, "I will wait for you here, and you can hang Auster's rein on the gate."

He looked at her doubtfully – "I will not be five minutes," he said.

"Oh, do not hurry yourself; Lizzie and I will not run away from you."

He hung my rein on one of the iron spikes, and was soon hidden among the trees. Lizzie was standing quietly by the side of the road a few paces off with her back to me. My young mistress was sitting easily with a loose rein, humming a little song. There was a meadow on the opposite side of the road, the gate of which stood open. Just then some cart horses and several young colts came trotting out in a very disorderly manner, while a boy behind was cracking a great whip. The colts were wild and frolicsome, and one of them bolted across the road, and blundered up against Lizzie's hind legs; and whether it was the stupid colt, or the loud cracking of the whip, or both together, I cannot say, but she gave a violent kick, and dashed off at a headlong gallop. It was so sudden that Lady Anne was nearly unseated. I gave a loud shrill neigh for help. Again and again I neighed, pawing the ground impatiently, and tossing my head to get the rein loose. I had not long to wait. Blantyre came running to the gate. He looked anxiously about, and just caught sight of the flying figure, now far away on the road. In an instant he sprang into the saddle. I needed no whip or spur, for I was as eager as my rider; he saw it, and gave me a free rein, and leaning a little forward, we dashed after them.

For about a mile and a half the road ran straight, and then turned to the right, after which it divided into two roads. Long before we came to the bend, she was out of sight. Which way had she turned? A woman was standing at her garden gate. Scarcely drawing the rein, Blantyre shouted, "Which way?" "To the right," cried the woman, and away we went up the right-hand road. For a moment we caught sight of her; and then – she was hidden again. Several times we caught glimpses of her but we scarcely seemed to gain ground at all.

An old road mender was standing near a heap of stones and as we came near he made a sign to speak. Blantyre drew the rein a little. "To the common, sir; she has turned off there." I knew this common very well. It was for the most part very uneven ground, covered with heather and dark green gorse bushes, with here and there a scrubby old thorn tree; there were ant hills and mole hills everywhere; the worst place I ever knew for a head-long gallop.

We hard hardly reached the common before we caught sight again of the green habit flying on before us. My lady's hat was gone, and her long brown hair was streaming behind her. Her head and body were thrown back, as if she were pulling with all her remaining strength, and as if that strength were nearly exhausted. It was clear that

119

the roughness of the ground had very much lessened Lizzie's speed, and there seemed a chance that we might overtake her.

While we were on the high road, Blantyre had given me my head; but now, with a light hand and a practised eye, he guided me over the ground in such a masterly manner, that my pace was scarcely slackened, and we were decidedly gaining on them.

About halfway across the heath there had been a wide ditch recently cut, and the earth from the cutting was cast up roughly on the other side. Surely this would stop them! But no; with scarcely a pause Lizzie took the leap, stumbled among the rough clods, and fell. Blantyre groaned. "Now, Auster, do your best!" He gave me a steady rein, I gathered myself well together, and with one determined leap cleared both ditch and bank.

Motionless among the heather, face downwards, lay my poor young mistress. Blantyre knelt down and called her name. Gently he turned her face upward; it was ghastly white, and the eyes were closed, "Annie, dear Annie, do speak!" but there was no answer. He unbuttoned her habit, loosened her collar, felt her hands and wrists, then started up and looked wildly around for help.

Two men now came running up; they had been cutting turf, and seeing Lizzie running wild without a rider had left their work to catch her. The first man seemed much troubled at the sight, and asked what he could do.

"Can you ride?"

"Well, sir, I bean't much of a horseman, but I'd risk my neck for Lady Anne; she was uncommon good to my wife in the winter."

"You'll be quite safe on this horse. Ride to the Doctor's and ask him to come instantly – then on to the Hall –

give them the news and tell them to send me the carriage
with Lady Anne's maid. I shall stay here."

"All right, sir, I'll do my best, and I pray God she's not
badly hurt. Here, Joe, run for some water, and tell my
missis to come as quick as she can to the Lady Anne."

He then somehow scrambled into the saddle, and with
a "Gee up" and a clap on my sides with both his legs, he
started on his journey, making a little circuit to avoid the
ditch. He had no whip, which seemed to trouble him, but
my pace soon cured that difficulty, and he found the best
thing he could do was to stick to the saddle, and hold me
in, which he did manfully. I shook him as little as I
could help, but once or twice on the rough ground he
called out, "Steady! Whoa! Steady!" On the high road
we were all right, and at the Doctors' and the Hall he did

his errand like a good man and true. They asked him in to take a drop of something. "No! no," he said, "I'll be back to 'em again by a short cut through the fields, and be there afore the carriage."

There was a great deal of hurry and excitement after the news became known. I was just turned into my box, the saddle and bridle were taken off, and a cloth thrown over me.

Ginger was saddled and sent off in great haste for Lord George, and I heard the carriage roll out of the yard.

It seemed a long time before Ginger came back and then she told me all that she had seen.

"I can't tell much" she said. "We went at a gallop nearly all the way, and got there just as the Doctor rode up. There was a woman sitting on the ground with the lady's head in her lap. The Doctor poured something into her mouth, but all that I heard was 'she is not dead.' After a while she was taken to the carriage, and we came home together. I heard my master tell a gentleman who stopped him to enquire that he hoped no bones were broken, but that she had not spoken yet."

Two days after the accident, Blantyre paid me a visit; he praised me very much and told Lord George that he was sure the horse knew of Annie's danger as well as he did. "I could not have held him in, if I had wanted to," said he, "She ought never to ride any other horse." I learned that my young mistress was now out of danger, and would soon be able to ride again. This was good news to me, and I looked forward to a happy life.

25. Reuben Smith

WHEN Lord George took Ginger for hunting, York shook his head; he said it ought to be a steady hand to train a horse for the first season, and not a hard rider like Lord George.

Ginger used to like it very much, but sometimes when she came back I could see that she had been very much strained, and now and then she gave a short cough. She had too much spirit to complain, but I could not help feeling anxious about her.

I must now say a little about Reuben Smith, who was left in charge of the stables when York went to London. No one understood his business more thoroughly than he did, and when he was all right, there could not be a more faithful or valuable man. He was gentle and very clever in his management of horses, and could doctor them almost as well as a farrier, for he had lived two years with a veterinary surgeon. Besides being an excellent driver he was a handsome man, a good scholar, and had very pleasant manners. I believe everybody liked him, but he had one great fault, and that was the love of drink. He was not like some men, always at it; he used to keep steady for weeks or months together, and then he would break out and have a "bout" of it, as York called it, and be a disgrace to himself, a terror to his wife, and a nuisance to everyone. He was so useful, however, that two or three times York had hushed the matter up, and kept it from the Earl's knowledge. But one night, when Reuben had to drive a party home from a ball, he was so drunk that he could not hold the reins, and a gentleman of the party had to drive the ladies home. Of course this could not be hidden, and Reuben was at once dismissed; his poor wife Susan and little children had to leave the pretty cottage by the Park gate and go where they could. Old Max told me all this, for it happened a good while ago; but shortly before Ginger and I came Smith had been taken back again. York had interceded for him with the Earl, who was very kindhearted, and the man had promised faithfully that he would never taste another drop as long as he lived there. He had kept his promise so well that York thought he might be safely trusted to fill his place while he was away.

It was now early in April, and the family would soon be home. The light brougham was to be freshly done up, and as Colonel Blantyre was due to return to his regiment, it was arranged that Smith should drive him to the town in it, and ride me back. At the station the Colonel put some money into Smith's hand and bade him good-bye, saying, "Take care of your young mistress, Reuben, and don't let Black Auster be hacked about by any young fool that wants to ride him – keep him for the lady."

We left the carriage at the maker's, and Smith rode me to the White Lion, and ordered the ostler to feed me well and have me ready for him at four o'clock. A nail in one of my front shoes had come loose as I came along, but the ostler did not notice it until just about four o'clock. Smith did not come into the yard until five, and then he said he would not leave until six, as he had met with some old friends. The man then told him of the nail, and asked if he should have the shoe seen to.

"No," said Smith, "that will be all right until we get home."

He spoke in a very loud offhand way, and I thought it very unlike him, not to see about loose nails in our shoes.

He did not come at six; it was nearly nine o'clock before he called for me, and then it was in a loud rough voice. He seemed in a very bad temper, and abused the ostler, though I could not tell what for.

The landlord stood at the door and said, "Be careful, Mr. Smith!" but he answered angrily with an oath; and almost before he was out of the town he began to gallop, frequently giving me a sharp cut with his whip, though I was going at full speed. The moon had not yet risen, and it was very dark. The roads were stony, having been recently mended; going over them at this pace my shoe became looser and when we were near the turnpike gate it came off.

If Smith had been in his right senses, he would have detected something wrong in my pace; but he was too madly drunk to notice anything.

Beyond the turnpike was a long piece of road, upon which fresh stones had just been laid; large sharp stones, over which no horse could safely go so fast. Over this road, with one shoe gone, I was forced to gallop at my utmost speed, my rider meanwhile cutting into me with his whip, and with wild curses urging me to go still faster. Of course my schoeless foot suffered dreadfully; the hoof was broken and split down to the very quick, and the inside was terribly cut by the sharpness of the stones.

No horse could keep his footing under such circumstances. Suddenly I stumbled, and fell violently on both my knees. Smith was flung off by my fall, and I was going so fast, he must have fallen with great force. I soon recovered my feet and limped to the side of the road, where it was free from stones. The moon had just risen above the hedge, and by its light I could see Smith lying a few yards beyond me. He made one slight effort to rise, and then there was a heavy groan. I could have groaned too, for I was suffering intense pain from my foot and both knees; but horses are used to bearing their pain in silence. Smith groaned again but though he now lay in the full moonlight, I could see no movement. I could do nothing for him nor myself. The road was not much used, and at this time of the night we might stay for hours before help came to us. I stood watching and listening. It was a calm sweet April night. There were no sounds but a few low notes of a nightingale, and nothing moved but the white clouds near the moon, and a brown owl that flitted over the hedge. It made me think of the summer nights long ago, when I used to lie beside my mother in the green pleasant meadow at Farmer Grey's.

26. How it Ended

IT must have been nearly midnight when I heard at a great distance the sound of a horse's feet. I was almost sure I could distinguish Ginger's step; a little nearer still, and I could tell she was in the dogcart. I neighed loudly, and was overjoyed to hear an answering neigh from Ginger, and men's voices. They came slowly over the stones, and stopped at the dark figure that lay upon the ground.

One of the men jumped out, and stooped down over it. "It is Reuben!" he said, "and he does not stir."

The other man followed and bent over him. "He's dead," he said.

They raised him up, but there was no life, and his hair was soaked with blood. They laid him down again, and came and looked at me. They soon saw my cut knees.

"Why, the horse has been down and thrown him! Who would have thought the black horse would have done that? Nobody thought he could fall. Reuben must have been lying here for hours! Odd, too, that the horse has not moved from the place."

Robert then attempted to lead me forward. I made a step, but almost fell again.

"Hullo! he's bad in his foot as well as his knees; look here – his hoof is cut all to pieces. No wonder he came down. Just think of Reuben riding a horse over these stones without a shoe! Why, if he had been in his right senses, he would just as soon have tried to ride him over the moon. I'm afraid it has been the old thing over again. Poor Susan! Now what must we do? There's the horse to get home as well as the body – and that will be no easy matter."

It was agreed that Robert, the groom, should lead me, and that Ned must take the body. It was a hard job to get it into the dogcart, but Ginger knew as well as I did what was going on, and stood as still as a stone.

Ned started off very slowly with his sad load, and Robert came and looked at my foot again; then he took his handkerchief and bound it closely around it and led me home. I shall never forget that night walk; it was more than three miles. Robert led me on very slowly, and I limped and hobbled on as well as I could with great pain. I am sure he was sorry for me, for he often patted and encouraged me, talking to me in a pleasant voice.

At last I reached my own box, and had some corn, and after Robert had wrapped up my knees in wet cloths, he tied up my foot in a bran poultice to draw out the heat, and cleanse it before the horse doctor saw it in the morning, and I managed to get myself down on the straw, and slept in spite of the pain.

The next day, after the farrier had examined my wounds, he said he hoped the joint was not injured, and if so, I should not be spoiled for work, but I should never lose the blemish. I believe they did the best to make a good cure, but it was a long and painful one; proud flesh, as they called it, came up in my knees, and was burned out with caustic, and when at last it was healed, they put a blistering fluid over the front of both knees to bring all the hair off. They had some reason for this, and I suppose it was all right.

At the inquest on Smith's death, the landlord and ostler at the White Lion, with several other people, gave evidence that he was intoxicated when he started from the inn. The keeper of the tollgate said he rode at a hard gallop through the gate; and my shoe was picked up among the stones, so that the case was quite plain to them, and I was cleared of all blame.

Everybody pitied Susan. She was nearly out of her mind: she kept saying over and over again, "Oh! he was so good – so good! it was all that cursed drink! why will they sell that cursed drink? Oh, Reuben, Reuben!" So she went on until after he was buried, and then, as she had no home or relations, she, with her six little children, was obliged once more to leave the pleasant home by the tall oak trees, and go into that great gloomy poorhouse.

27. Ruined, and Going Downhill

As soon as my knees were sufficiently healed, I was turned into a small meadow for a month or two; no other creature was there, and though I enjoyed the liberty and the sweet grass, yet I had been so long used to society that I felt very lonely. Ginger and I had become fast friends, and now I missed her company extremely. I often neighed when I heard horses' feet passing in the road, but I seldom got an answer, untill one morning the gate was opened, and who should come in but dear old Ginger. The man slipped off her halter and left her there. With a joyful whinny I trotted up to her. We were both glad to meet, but I soon found that it was not for our pleasure that she was brought to be with me. She had been ruined by hard riding, and was now turned out to see what rest would do for her.

Lord George was young and would take no warning. He was a hard rider, and would hunt whenever he could get the chance, quite careless of his horse. Soon after I left the stable there was a steeplechase, and he took part. Though the groom had told him Ginger was a little strained, and was not fit for the race, he did not believe it, and urged her to keep up with the foremost riders. She did her utmost and came in with the first three horses, but her wind was touched; beside which, he was too heavy for her, and her back was strained. "And so," she said, "here we are – ruined in the prime of our youth and strength – you by a drunkard, and I by a fool. It is very hard." But we enjoyed each other's company. We did not gallop about as we once had, but we used to eat, and lie down together, and stand for hours under one of the shady lime trees with our heads close to each other; and so we passed our time until the family returned from town.

One day we saw the Earl come into the meadow, and York was with him. They examined us carefully. The Earl seemed much annoyed.

"There is three hundred pounds flung away for no earthly use," said he. "But what I mind most is that these horses of my old friend, who thought they would find a good home with me, are ruined. The mare shall have a twelvemonth's rest, and we shall see what that will do for her; but the black one must be sold. 'Tis a great pity, but I could not have knees like these in my stables."

"No, my lord, of course not," said York, "but he might

get a place where appearance is not of much consequence, and still be well treated. I know a man in Bath, the master of some livery stables, who likes a bargain. He looks after his horses very well.'

"You had better write to him, York. I should be more particular about the place than the money he would bring."

After this they left us.

"They'll soon take you away," said Ginger, "and I shall lose the only friend I have, and most likely we shall never see each other again. 'Tis a hard world!"

About a week after this, Robert came into the field and led me away. Ginger neighed as I was led off, and trotted anxiously along by the hedge calling to me as long as she could hear the sound of my feet.

I had been sold to the master of the livery stables. I had to go by train, which was new to me, and required a good deal of courage the first time; but as I found the puffing, rushing, whistling, and, more than all, the trembling of the horsebox in which I stood did me no real harm, I soon took it quietly.

When I reached the end of my journey, I found myself in a tolerably comfortable stable and well attended to. These stables were not as airy and pleasant as those I had been used to. The stalls were laid on a slope instead of being level, and as my head was kept tied to the manger, I was obliged always to stand on the slope, which was very fatiguing. However, I was well fed and well cleaned, and, on the whole, I think our master took as much care of us as he could. He kept a good many horses and carriages of different kinds, for hire. Sometimes his own men drove them; at others, the horse and chaise were let to gentlemen or ladies who drove themselves.

28. A Job Horse and his Drivers

HITHERTO I had always been driven by people who at least knew how to drive; but now I was a "job horse", and was let out to all sorts of people who wished to hire me; and as I was good-tempered and gentle, I think I was oftener let out to the ignorant drivers than some of the other horses, because I could be depended upon. As a result I learned about the different kinds of bad driving to which we horses are subjected.

First, there are the tightrein drivers – men who seem to think that all depends on holding the reins as hard as they can, never relaxing the pull on the horse's mouth, or giving him the least liberty of movement. Some poor broken-down horses, whose mouths have been made hard and insensible by just such drivers as these, may, perhaps, find some support in this, but for a horse who can depend upon its own legs, and who has a tender mouth, and is easily guided, it is not only tormenting, but stupid.

Then there are the loose rein drivers, who let the reins lie easily on our backs, and their own hand rest lazily on their knees. Of course, they have no control over a horse in an emergency. If a horse shies, or starts, or stumbles, they are nowhere and cannot help the horse or themselves, until the mischief is done. For myself, I had no objection to it, as I was not in the habit of starting or stumbling, and all I wanted from my driver was guidance and encouragement. Still, one likes to feel the rein a little in going downhill, and know that the driver has not gone to sleep.

Besides, a slovenly way of driving gets a horse into lazy habits; and when he changes hands, he has to be whipped out of them with pain and trouble. Squire Gordon always kept us to our best paces, and our best manners. He said that spoiling a horse and letting him get into bad habits was just as cruel as spoiling a child, and both had to suffer for it afterwards.

Many drivers are careless, and will attend to anything else rather than their horses. I went out in the phaeton one day with one of them. He had a lady and two children

behind. He flopped the reins about as we started, and of course gave me several unmeaning cuts with the whip, though I was going well. There had been a good deal of road-mending going on, and there were a great many loose stones about. My driver was laughing and joking with his family, and talking about the countryside; but he never thought it worthwhile to keep an eye on his horse or to drive on the smoothest parts of the road, and so it easily happened that I got a stone in one of my feet.

Now any good driver would have seen at once that something was wrong. Even in the dark, a practised hand would have felt by the rein that there was something wrong in the step, and would have got down and picked out the stone. But this man went on laughing and talking, while at every step the stone became more firmly wedged between my shoe and the frog of my foot. The stone was sharp on the inside and round on the outside, which is the most dangerous kind that a horse can pick up; at the same time cutting his foot, and making him liable to stumble and fall.

Whether the man was partly blind, or only very careless, I can't say; but he drove me with that stone in my foot for a good half mile before he saw anything. By that time I was going so lame with the pain that at last he saw it and called out, "Well, here's a poor thing! Why, they have sent us out with a lame horse! What a shame!"

He then chucked the reins and flipped about with the whip, saying, "Now, then, it's no use playing the old soldier with me; there's the journey to do and it's no use turning lame and lazy."

Just then a farmer came riding up on a brown cob. He lifted his hat and pulled up.

"I beg your pardon, sir," he said, "but I think there is something the matter with your horse; he goes very much as if he had a stone in his shoe. If you will allow me, I will look at his feet; these loose scattered stones are confounded dangerous things for the horses."

"He's a hired horse," said my driver. "I don't know

what's the matter with him, but it's a great shame to send out a lame beast like this."

The farmer dismounted, and slipping his rein over his arm, at once took up my near foot.

"Bless me, there's a stone! Lame! I should think so!"

As it was now very tightly wedged, he drew a stone-pick out of his pocket, and very carefully, and with some trouble, got it out. Then holding it up, he said, "There, that's the stone your horse had picked up; it is a wonder he did not fall down and break his knees."

"That is a queer thing!" said my driver, "I never knew that horses picked up stones before!"

"Didn't you?" said the farmer, rather contemptuously. "They do, though, and the best of them can't help it, on such roads as these. And if you don't want to lame your horse, you must get them out quickly. This foot is very much bruised," he said, setting it gently down and patting me. "If I might advise, sir, you had better drive him gently for a while; the foot is badly hurt, and the lameness will not go off immediately."

Then, mounting his cob and raising his hat to the lady, he trotted off.

When he was gone, my driver began to flop the reins about, and whip the harness, by which I understood that I was to go on, which of course I did, glad that the stone was gone, but still in a good deal of pain.

This was the sort of experience we job horses often came in for.

29. Steam Engine Drivers

THEN there is the steam engine style of driving; these drivers are mostly people from towns, who never had a horse of their own, and generally travel by rail.

They always seem to think that a horse is something like a steam engine, only smaller. At any rate, they think that if they pay for it, a horse is bound to go just as far, and just as fast, and with just as heavy a load as they please, whatever the state of the roads.

These people never think of getting out to walk up a steep hill. They have paid to ride, and ride they will! The horse? Oh, he's used to it! And so the whip is plied and the rein is chucked, and often a rough scolding voice cries out, "Go along, you lazy beast!" And all the time we are doing our very best to get along, uncomplaining and obedient, though often harassed and downhearted.

This steam engine style of driving wears us out faster than any other kind. I would far rather go twenty miles with a good considerate driver, than ten with some of these.

They scarcely ever put on the brake, however steep the downhill may be, and thus bad accidents sometimes happen; or if they do put it on, they often forget to take it off at the bottom of the hill. More than once I have had to pull halfway up the next hill, with one of the wheels lodged fast in the brake shoe, before my driver thought about it; and that is a terrible strain on a horse.

Then these townspeople, instead of starting at an easy pace as a countryman would do, generally set off at full speed from the very stable yard; and when they want to stop, they first whip us and then pull up so suddenly, that we are nearly thrown on our haunches, and our mouths jagged with the bit. When they turn a corner, they do it as if there were no right or wrong side of the road.

I well remember one spring evening after Rory and I had been out for the day. (Rory was the horse that usually went with me when a pair was ordered, and a good honest fellow he was.) We had our own driver, and as he was always considerate and gentle with us, we had a very pleasant day. We were coming home at a good smart pace about twilight. Our road turned sharp to the left, but as we were close to the hedge on our own side, and there was plenty of room to pass, our driver did not pull us in. As we neared the corner I heard a horse and two wheels coming rapidly down the hill towards us. The hedge was high and I could see nothing, but the next moment we were upon each other. Happily for me, I was on the side next the hedge. Rory was on the right side of the pole, and had not even a shaft to protect him. The man who was driving was making straight for the corner, and when he came in sight of us he had no time to pull over to his own side. The whole shock came upon Rory. The gig shaft ran right into the chest, making him stagger back with a cry that I shall never forget. The other horse was thrown upon his haunches, and one shaft broken. It turned out that it was a horse from our own stables, with the high-wheeled gig that the young men liked.

The driver was one of those careless ignorant fellows, who don't even know which is their own side of the road, or if they know, don't care. And there was poor Rory with his chest torn open and bleeding, and the blood streaming down. They said if it had been a little more to one side it would have killed him.

As it was, it was a long time before the wound healed, and then he was sold for coal carting; and what that is, up and down those steep hills, only horses know. Some of the sights I saw there, where a horse had to come downhill with a heavily loaded two-wheel cart behind him, on which no brake could be placed, make me sad to think of.

After Rory was disabled, I often went in the carriage with a mare named Peggy. She was a strong, well-made animal, of a bright dun colour, beautifully dappled, and with a dark brown mane and tail. There was no high breeding about her, but she was very pretty, and remarkably sweet-tempered and willing. Still, there was an anxious look about her eye, by which I knew that she had some trouble. The first time we went out together I thought she had a very odd pace; she seemed to go partly in a trot, partly in a canter – three or four paces, and then a little jump forward. It was very unpleasant for any horse who pulled with her, and made me quite fidgety. When we got home, I asked her what made her go in that odd, awkward way.

"Ah," she said in a troubled manner, "I know my paces are very bad, but what can I do? It is just because my legs are so short. I stand nearly as high as you, but your legs are a good three inches longer above your knees than mine, and of course you can take a much longer step, and go much faster. You see, I did not make myself; I wish I could have done so, I would have had long legs then," said Peggy, in a despondent tone.

"But how is it," I said, "when you are so strong and good-tempered and willing?'

"Why, you see," said she, "men will go so fast, and if one can't keep up with other horses, it is nothing but whip, whip, whip, all the time. And so I have had to keep up as I could, and have got into this ugly shuffling pace. It was not always so; when I lived with my first master I always went a good regular trot, but then he was not in such a hurry. He was a young clergyman in the country, and a good kind master he was. He never scolded or whipped me for not going faster. I only wish I was with him now; but he had to leave and then I was sold to a farmer.

"Some farmers, you know, are the best of masters; but I think this one was a low sort of man. He cared nothing about good horses, or good driving; he only cared for going fast. I went as fast as I could, but that would not do, and he was always whipping; so I got into this way of making a spring forward to keep up.

"On market nights he used to stay very late at the inn, and then drive home at a gallop. One dark night he was galloping home as usual, when all of a sudden the wheel came against some obstruction in the road, and turned the gig over. He was thrown out and his arm broken, and some of his ribs. It was the end of my living with him. But you see it will be the same everywhere for me, if men *must* go so fast. I wish my legs were longer!"

She was often used in the phaeton, and was very much liked by ladies, because she was so gentle; and later she was sold to two ladies who drove themselves, and wanted a safe good horse. I met her several times and I was very glad to see her, for she deserved a good home.

After she left us, another horse took her place. He was young, and had a bad name for shying and starting. I asked him what made him shy.

"Well, I hardly know," he said, "I was timid when I was young, and if I saw anything strange, I used to turn and look at it – you see, with our blinkers on one can't see what a thing is unless one looks around, and then my master always whipped me, which of course did not make me less afraid. I think if he would have let me just look at things quietly, and see that there was nothing to hurt me, it would have been all right and I would have got used to them. One day an old gentleman was riding with him, and a large piece of white paper blew across just on one side of me. I shied and started forward – my master as usual whipped me smartly, but the old man cried out, 'You're wrong! You should never whip a horse for shying. He shies because he is frightened, and you only frighten him more, and make the habit worse.' I am sure I don't want to shy for the sake of it; but how can one know what is dangerous and what is not, if one is never allowed to get used to anything? I am never afraid of what I know. Now I was brought up in a park where there were deer. Of course, I knew them as well as I did a sheep or a cow, but they are not common, and I know many sensible horses who are frightened of them, and who kick up quite a row before they will pass a paddock where there are deer."

I knew what my companion said was true, and I wished that every young horse had as good a master as Farmer Grey and Squire Gordon.

Of course we sometimes came in for good driving here. I remember one morning I was put into the light gig, and taken to a house in Pulteney Street. Two gentlemen came out. The taller of them came around to my head, he looked at the bit and bridle, and shifted the collar with his hand.

"Do you consider this horse needs a curb?" he said to the ostler.

"Well," said the man, "I should say he would go just as well without, he has an uncommon good mouth, and though he has a fine spirit, he has no vice; but we generally find people like the curb."

"I don't like it," said the gentleman. "Please, put the rein in at the cheek. An easy mouth is a great thing on a long journey, is it not, old fellow?" he said.

Then he took the reins, and they both got up. I can remember now how quietly he turned me around, and then with a light feel of the rein, and drawing the whip gently across my back, we were off.

I arched my neck and set off at my best pace. I found I had some one behind me who knew how a good horse ought to be driven. It seemed like old times again, and made me feel quite gay.

This gentleman took a great liking to me, and prevailed upon my master to sell me to a friend of his, who wanted a safe pleasant horse for riding. And so in the summer I was sold to Mr. Barry.

30. A Thief

M Y new master was an unmarried business man at Bath,
His doctor advised him to take horse exercise, and he
bought me for this purpose. He hired a stable a short
distance from his lodgings, and engaged a man named
Filcher as groom. My master knew very little about horses, but he treated me well, and I would have had a good
and easy place, but for circumstances of which he was ignorant. He ordered the best hay with plenty of oats, crushed
beans, and bran, with vetches, or rye grass, as the man
might think needful. I heard the master give the order, so
I knew there was plenty of good food, and I thought I
was well off.

For a few days all went on well. I found that my
groom understood his business. He kept the stable clean
and airy, and he groomed me thoroughly, and was always
gentle. He had been an ostler and now cultivated fruit
and vegetables for the market, and his wife bred poultry
and rabbits for sale.

After a while it seemed to me that I did not get as many
oats as usual. In two or three weeks this began to tell
upon my strength and spirits. I had the grass food, but
though very good, it was not the thing to keep up my
condition without oats. However, I could not complain,
nor make known my wants. So it went on for about two
months; and I wondered my master did not see that
something was the matter. However, one afternoon he
rode out into the country to see a friend of his. This
gentleman had a very quick eye for horses; and after he
had welcomed his friend, he said, casting his eye over me:

"It seems to me, Barry, that your horse does not look

so well as he did when you first had him. Has he been well?"

"Yes, I believe so," said my master, "but he is not nearly so lively as he was. My groom tells me that horses are always dull and weak in the autumn, and that I must expect it."

"Autumn! fiddlesticks!" said the farmer. "Why, this is only August, and with your light work and good food he ought not to go down like this, even if it was autumn. How do you feed him?"

My master told him. The other shook his head slowly, and began to feel me over.

"I can't say who eats your oats, my dear fellow, but I doubt if your horse gets them. Have you ridden very fast?"

"No! very gently."

"Then just put your hand here," said he, passing his hand over my neck and shoulder. "He is as warm and damp as a horse just come up from grass. I advise you to look into your stable a little more. I hate to be suspicious, but there are mean scoundrels, wicked enough to rob a dumb beast of his food." And turning to his man who had come to take me: "Give this horse a good feed of bruised oats, and don't stint him."

"Dumb beasts!" yes, we are, but if I could have spoken, I could have told my master where his oats went to. My groom used to come every morning about six o'clock, and with him a little boy, who always had a covered basket with him. He used to go with his father into the harness room where the oats were kept, and I could see him when the door stood ajar, fill a bag with oats out of the bin and then be off.

Five or six mornings later, just as the boy had left the stable, the door was pushed open and a policeman walked in, holding the child tight by the arm. Another policeman followed, and locked the door on the inside, saying, "Show me the place where your father keeps his rabbits' food."

The boy looked very frightened and began to cry; but there was no escape, and he led the way to the cornbin. Here the policeman found another empty bag like that which was found full of oats in the boy's basket.

Filcher blustered a good deal, but they walked him off to the "lock-up." He was sent to prison for two months.

31. A Humbug

In a few days my new groom came. He was a tall, good-looking fellow enough; but if ever there was a humbug, Alfred Smirk was the man. He was very civil to me, and never used me ill. In fact, he did a great deal of stroking and patting, when his master was there to see it. He always brushed my mane and tail with water, and my hoofs with oil before he brought me to the door, to make me look smart, but as to cleaning my feet, or looking to my shoes, or grooming me thoroughly, he thought no more of that than if I had been a cow. He left my bit rusty, my saddle damp, and my crupper stiff.

Alfred Smirk considered himself very handsome. He spent a great deal of time before a little looking glass in the harness room. When his master was speaking to him, it was always, "Yes, sir, yes, sir", touching his hat at every word, and everyone thought he was a very nice young man, and that Mr. Barry was very fortunate to meet with him. I would say he was the laziest, most conceited fellow I ever came near. I had a loose box, and might have been very comfortable if he had not been too indolent to clean it out. He never took all the straw away, and the smell from what lay underneath was very bad, while the strong fumes that rose up made my eyes inflamed, and took away my appetite for my food.

One day his master came in and said, "Alfred, the stable smells rather strong; should not you give that stall a good scrub, and throw down plenty of water?"

"Well, sir," he said, touching his cap, "I'll do so if you please, sir, but it is rather dangerous, sir, throwing down water in a horse's box, they are very apt to take cold, sir. I should not like to do him an injury, but I'll do it if you please, sir."

"Well," said his master, "I should not like him to take cold but I don't like the smell of this stable. Do you think the drains are all right?"

"Well, sir, now you mention it, I think the drain does sometimes send back a smell. There may be something wrong, sir."

"Then send for the bricklayer and have it seen to," said his master.

"Yes, sir, I will."

The bricklayer came and pulled up a great many bricks, and found nothing wrong; so he put down some lime and charged the master five shillings, and the smell in my box was as bad as ever. But that was not all. Standing as I did on a quantity of moist straw, my feet grew unhealthy and tender, and the master used to say,

"I don't know what is the matter with this horse, he goes very fumble-footed. I am sometimes afraid he will stumble."

"Yes, sir," said Alfred, "I have noticed the same myself, when I have exercised him."

Now the fact was, that he hardly ever did exercise me, and when the master was busy, I often stood for days, without stretching my legs at all, and yet being fed just

as high as if I were at hard work. This made me sometimes heavy and dull, but more often restless and feverish.
He never even gave me a meal of green meat, or a bran
mash, which would have cooled me. Instead of exercise
or change of food, I had to take horse pills and medicine,
which, beside the nuisance of having them poured down
my throat, used to make me feel ill and uncomfortable.

One day my feet were so tender, that trotting over some
stones with my master on my back, I made two bad
stumbles. As he came down Lansdown into the city, he
stopped at the farrier's, and asked him to see what was
the matter with me. The man took up my feet one by one
and examined them.

"Your horse," he said, "has got the 'thrush', and badly
too; his feet are very tender; it is fortunate that he has
not fallen down. I wonder your groom has not seen to it
before. This is the sort of thing we find in foul stables,
where the litter is never properly cleared out. If you will
send him here tomorrow, I will attend to the hoof, and I
will direct your man how to apply the liniment which I
will give him."

The next day I had my feet thoroughly cleaned and
stuffed with tow, soaked in some strong lotion – and a
very unpleasant business it was.

The farrier ordered all the litter to be taken out of my
box day by day, and the floor kept very clean. Then I was
to have bran mashes, a little green meat, and not so much
corn, until my feet were well again. With this treatment
I soon regained my spirits, but Mr. Barry was so much
disgusted at being twice deceived by his grooms that he
determined to give up keeping a horse, and to hire when
he wanted one. I was therefore kept until my feet were
quite sound, and was then sold again.

32. A Horse Fair

I WAS sold at a horse fair, with hundreds of other horses.

Young horses out of the country, fresh from the marshes; shaggy little Welsh ponies, no higher than Merrylegs; cart horses of all sorts, some of them with their long tails braided up, and tied with scarlet cord; and a good many like myself, handsome and highbred, but fallen into the middle class, through some accident or blemish, unsoundness of wind, or some other complaint. There were some splendid animals still in their prime, and fit for anything. They were showing off their paces in high style, as they were trotted out with a leading rein, the groom running by the side. But in the background there were a number of poor things, sadly broken down with hard work, with their knees knuckling over, and their hind legs swinging out at every step. There were some very dejected-looking old horses, with their underlips hanging down, and their ears laying back heavily, as if there was no more pleasure in life, and no more hope. There were some so thin, you might see all their ribs, and some with old sores on their backs and hips. These are sad sights for a horse to look upon who knows he may come to the same state.

There was a great deal of bargaining, of running up and beating down, and I should say there was a great deal of lying and trickery. I was put with two or three other strong, useful-looking horses, and a good many people came to look at us. The gentlemen always turned from me when they saw my broken knees, though the man who had me swore it was only a slip in the stall.

The first thing was to pull my mouth open, then to look at my eyes, then feel all the way down my legs, and give

me a hard feel of the skin and flesh, and then try my paces. It was wonderful what a difference there was in the way these things were done. Some did it in a rough off-hand way, as if I was only a piece of wood; while others would move their hands gently over my body, with a pat now and then, as much as to say, "by your leave."

There was one man I thought I should like to be bought by. He was not a gentleman, nor yet one of the loud flashy sort that called themselves so. He was rather a small man, but well made, and quick in all his motions. I knew in a moment, by the way he handled me, that he was used to horses; he spoke gently, and his gray eye had a kindly, cheery look in it. The clean fresh smell there was about him made me take to him; no smell of old beer and tobacco, which I hated, but a fresh smell as if he had come out of a hayloft. He offered twenty-three pounds for me; but that was refused, and he walked away. Several other men made bids for me, which were also refused, and then the gray-eyed man came back. I could not help reaching out my head towards him. He stroked my face kindly.

"Well, old chap," he said, "I think we would suit each other. I'll give twenty-four for him."

"Say twenty-five and you shall have him."

"Twenty-four ten," said my friend, in a very decided tone, "and not another sixpence – yes or no?"

"Done," said the salesman, "and you may depend upon it there's a lot of quality in that horse, and if you want him for cab work, he's a bargain."

The money was paid on the spot, and my new master led me to an inn, where he had a saddle and bridle ready. He gave me a good meal of oats, and stood by while I ate it, talking to himself and talking to me. Half-an-hour after, we were on our way to London, through pleasant lanes and country roads, until we came into the main London road, on which we went steadily, until in the twilight we reached the great city. The gas lamps were already lighted; there were streets to the right, and streets to the left, and streets crossing each other for mile upon mile. I thought we would never come to the end of them. At last, we came to a long cab stand, and my rider called out in a cheery voice, "Good night, Governor!"

"Good night!" cried a voice, "have you got a good one?"

"I think so," replied my owner.

"I wish you luck with him."

"Thank ye, Governor," and he rode on. We soon turned up one of the side streets, and about halfway up that, we turned into a very narrow street, with rather poor-looking houses on one side, and what seemed to be coach houses and stables on the other.

My owner pulled up at one of the houses and whistled. The door flew upon, and a young woman, followed by a little girl and boy, ran out. There was a very lively greeting as my rider dismounted.

"Harry, my boy, open the gates, and mother will bring us the lantern."

The next minute they were all standing around me in a small stable yard.

"Is he gentle, father?"

"Yes, Dolly, as gentle as your own kitten; come and pat him."

At once the little hand was patting about all over my shoulder without fear. How good it felt!

"Let me get him a bran mash while you rub him down," said the mother.

"Do, Polly, it's just what he wants."

33. A London Cab Horse

MY new master's name was Jeremiah Barker, but as every one called him Jerry, I shall do the same. Polly, his wife, was a plump, trim, tidy little woman, with smooth dark hair, dark eyes, and a merry little mouth. Harry was nearly twelve, a tall, frank, good-tempered lad; and little Dorothy (Dolly they called her) was her mother over again, at eight years old. They were all wonderfully fond of each other; I never knew such a happy family before, or since. Jerry had a cab of his own, and two horses, which he drove and attended to himself. His other horse was a tall, white, rather large-boned animal, called Captain. He was old now, but when he was young he must have been splendid and he was still a highbred, fine-mannered, noble old horse.

The next morning, when I was well groomed, Polly and Dolly came into the yard to see me, and make friends. Harry had been helping his father since the early morning, and we were already friends. Polly brought me a slice of apple, and Dolly a piece of bread, and made as much of me as if I had been the "Black Beauty" of old. It was a great treat to be petted again, and talked to in a gentle voice. Polly thought I was very handsome, and a great deal too good for a cab, except for the broken knees.

"Of course, we don't know whose fault that was," said Jerry, "and I shall give him the benefit of the doubt; for a firmer, neater stepper I never rode. We'll call him 'Jack', after the old one – shall we, Polly?"

"Do," she said, "for I like to keep a good name going."

Captain went out in the cab all the morning. Harry came in after school to feed and water me. In the afternoon I was put into the cab. Jerry took as much pains as John Manly to see if the collar and bridle fitted comfortably. When the crupper was let out a hole or two, it all fitted well. There was no bearing rein – no curb – nothing but a plain ring snaffle. What a blessing that was!

After driving through the side street we came to the large cab stand where Jerry had said "Good night". On one side of this wide street were high houses with wonderful shop fronts, and on the other was an old church and churchyard surrounded by iron railings. Alongside these railings a number of cabs were drawn up, waiting for passengers: bits of hay were lying about on the ground; some of the men were standing together, some were sitting on their boxes reading the newspaper; and one or two were feeding and watering their horses. We pulled up in the rank at the back of the last cab. Two or three men came around and began to look at me and pass remarks.

"Very good for a funeral," said one.

"Too smart-looking," said another, shaking his head solemnly; "you'll find out something wrong one of these fine mornings, or my name isn't Jones."

"Well," said Jerry pleasantly, "I suppose I need not find it out until it finds me out, eh? and so I'll keep up my spirits a little longer."

Then came up a broad-faced man, dressed in a great gray coat with great gray capes, and great white buttons, a gray hat, and a blue comforter loosely tied around his neck; his hair was gray too, but he was a jolly-looking fellow. He looked me all over, then said, "He's the right sort for you, Jerry; I don't care what you gave for him, he'll be worth it." Thus my character was established on the stand.

This man's name was Grant and he was called "Governor Grant". He had been longer than anyone else on that stand and he took it upon himself to settle matters, and stop disputes. He was generally a good tempered, sensible man; but when he was angry, as he was sometimes, when he had drunk too much, nobody liked to come too near his fist, for he could give a very heavy blow.

The first week of my life as a cab horse was very trying. I had never been used to London, and the noise, the hurry, the crowds of horses, carts, and carriages that I had to make my way through made me feel anxious and harassed. But I soon found that I could trust my driver perfectly, and then I made myself easy, and got used to it.

Jerry was as good a driver as I had ever known and took as much thought for his horses as he did for himself. He soon found out that I was willing to do my best, he never laid the whip on me, unless it was gently drawing the end of it over my back, when I was to go on. Even this was seldom necessary.

In a short time he and I understood each other as well as horse and man can do. In the stable, too, he did all that he could for our comfort. The stalls were the old-fashioned style, too much on the slope, but he had two movable bars fixed across the back of our stalls, so that at night, and when we were resting, he just took off our halters, and put up the bars, and thus we could turn about and stand whichever way we pleased, which was a great comfort.

Jerry kept us very clean, and gave us as much change of food as he could, and always plenty of it; and plenty of clean fresh water, which he allowed to stand by us both night and day, except of course when we came in warm. Some people say that a horse ought not to drink all he likes, but I know if we are allowed to drink when we want it, we drink only a little at a time, and it does us a great deal more good than swallowing down half a bucket full at a time because we have been left without until we are thirsty and miserable. Some grooms will go home to their beer and leave us for hours with our dry hay and oats, and nothing to moisten them; then of course we gulp down too much at once, which helps to spoil our breathing and sometimes chills our stomachs.

But the best thing that we had here was our Sundays for rest. We worked so hard in the week, that I do not think we could have kept up to it, but for that day; besides, we had then time to enjoy each other's company. It was on these days that I learned my companion's history.

34. An Old War Horse

IN youth Captain had been a dark, dappled iron gray, and considered very handsome. He had been an army horse. His first owner was a cavalry officer going out to the Crimean War. His master, a young, high-spirited gentleman, was very fond of him, and treated him from the first with the greatest care and kindness. He thought the life of an army horse was very pleasant, but when he came to be sent abroad, over the sea in a great ship, he almost changed his mind.

"That part of it," said he, "was dreadful! To get us on board they were obliged to put strong straps under our bodies, and then we were lifted off our legs, and swung through the air over the water, to the deck of the great vessel. There we were placed in small close stalls, and for a long time never saw the sky, or were able to stretch our legs. The ship sometimes rolled about in high winds, and we were knocked about. However, at last it came to an end, and we were hauled up and swung over again to the land. We were very glad, and snorted, and neighed for joy, when we once more felt firm ground under our feet.

"We soon found that the country we had come to was very different from our own, and that we had many hardships to endure besides the fighting; but many of the men were so fond of their horses that they did everything they could to make them comfortable, in spite of snow and wet."

"But what about the fighting?" said I. "Was not that worse than anything else?"

"Well," said he, "I hardly know. We always liked to hear the trumpet sound, and to be called out, and were impatient to start off, though sometimes we had to stand for hours, waiting for the word of command; and when the word was given, we used to spring forward as gaily and eagerly as if there were no cannon balls or bullets. I believe so long as we felt out rider firm in the saddle, and his hand steady on the bridle, not one of us gave way to fear, not even when the terrible shells whirled through the air and burst into a thousand pieces.

"My master and I went into many actions together without a wound, and though I saw horses shot down with bullets, pierced through with lances, and gashed with fearful sabre cuts, I don't think I feared for myself. My master's voice, as he encouraged his men, made me feel as if he and I could not be killed. I had such perfect trust in him that while he was guiding me, I was ready to charge up to the very cannon's mouth. I saw many brave men killed or mortally wounded. I had heard the cries of the dying, I had cantered over ground slippery with blood, and frequently had to turn aside to avoid trampling on wounded men or horses, but I had never felt terror until one dreadful day, that I shall never forget."

Here old Captain paused for a while and drew a long breath; I waited, and he went on.

"It was one autumn morning, and as usual, an hour before daybreak our cavalry had turned out, ready for the day's work, whatever it might be. The men stood by their horses waiting, ready for orders. As the light increased, there seemed to be some excitement among the officers; and before the day was well begun, we heard the firing of the enemy's guns.

"Then one of the officers rode up and gave the word for the men to mount, and in a second, every man was in his saddle, and every horse stood eagerly expecting the touch of the rein, or the pressure of his rider's heels, but so well trained that, except for the champing of our bits, and the restive tossing of our heads from time to time, it could not be said that we stirred.

"My master and I were at the head of the line, and as all sat motionless and watchful, he took a little stray lock of my mane which had turned over on the wrong side, laid it over on the right, and smoothed it down with his hand; then patting my neck, he said, 'We shall have a day of it today, Bayard, my beauty; but we'll do our duty as we have done.' I loved to feel his hand on my neck, and arched my crest proudly and happily, but I stood very still, for I knew all his moods, and when he liked me to be quiet, and when gay.

"I cannot tell all that happened on that day, but I will tell of the last charge that we made together: it was across a valley right in front of the enemy's cannon. By this time we were well used to the roar of heavy guns, the rattle of musket fire, and the flying of shot near us; but never had I been under such a fire as we rode through on that day. From the right, from the left, and from the front, shot and shell poured in upon us. Many a brave man went down, many a horse fell, flinging his rider to the earth; many a horse without a rider ran wildly out of the ranks, then terrified at being alone with no hand to guide him, came pressing in among his old companions, to gallop with them to the charge.

"Fearful as it was, no one stopped, no one turned back. Every moment the ranks were thinned, but as our comrades fell, we closed in to keep together, and instead of being shaken or staggered in our pace, our gallop became faster and faster as we neared the cannon, all clouded in white smoke, while the red fire flashed through it.

159

"My master was cheering on his comrades, when one of the balls, whizzing close to my head, struck him. I felt him stagger with the shock, though he uttered no cry. I tried to check my speed, but the sword dropped from his right hand, the rein fell loose from the left, and he fell to the earth; the other riders swept past us, and by the force of their charge I was driven from the spot where he fell.

"I wanted to keep my place by his side, and not leave him under that rush of horses' feet, but it was in vain; and now, without a master or a friend, I was alone on that great slaughter ground. Fear took hold of me, and I trembled as I had never trembled before. Just then, a soldier whose horse had been killed under him caught at my bridle and mounted me; and with this new master I went forward again; but our gallant company had lost too heavily, and those who remained alive after the fierce fight for the guns came galloping back over the same ground. Some of the horses had been so badly wounded that they could scarcely move, others were trying to drag themselves along on three legs, and others were struggling to rise on their fore feet, when their hind legs had been shattered by shot. Their groans were piteous to hear, and the beseeching look in their eyes as those who escaped passed by, and left them to their fate, I shall never forget. After the battle the wounded men were brought in".

"And what about the wounded horses?" I said. "Were they left to die?"

"No, the army farriers went over the field with their pistols, and shot all that were ruined. Some that had only slight wounds were brought back and attended to, but the greater part of my friends that went out that morning never came back! In our stables there was only about one in four that returned. I never saw my dear master again. I never loved any other master so well."

I said, "I have heard people talk about war as if it was a very fine thing."

"Ah!" said he, "I should think they never saw it. No doubt it is very fine when there is no enemy, when it is just exercise and parade, and sham fight; but when thousands of good brave men and horses are killed, or crippled for life, it has a very different look."

"Do you know what they fought about?" said I.

"No," he said. "That is more than a horse can understand, but the enemy must have been awfully wicked people, if it was right to go all that way over the sea on purpose to kill them."

35. Jerry Barker

I NEVER knew a better man than my new master. He was kind and good, and as strong for the right as John Manly, and so good-tempered and merry that very few people could pick a quarrel with him. He was very fond of making little songs, and singing them to himself. One he liked very much was this:

> Come, father and mother,
> And sister and brother,
> Come, all of you, turn to
> And help one another.

And so they did; Harry was as clever at stable work as a much older boy, and always wanted to do what he could. Then Polly and Dolly used to come in the morning to brush and beat the cushions, and rub the glass, while Jerry was giving us a cleaning in the yard, and Harry was rubbing the harness. There used to be a great deal of laughing and fun between them, and it put Captain and me in very good spirits. They were always early in the morning, for Jerry would say:

> If you in the morning
> Throw minutes away
> You can't pick them up
> In the course of the day.
> You may hurry and skurry,
> And flurry and worry,
> You've lost them for ever,
> For ever and aye.

He could not bear any waste of time, and nothing was so near making him angry as to find people who were always late, wanting a cab horse to be driven hard, to make up for their idleness.

One day, two wild-looking young men came out of a tavern close by the stand, and called Jerry.

"Here, cabby! look sharp, we are rather late. Put on the steam, will you, and take us to Victoria in time for the one o'clock train? You shall have a shilling extra."

"I will take you at the regular pace, gentlemen. Shillings don't pay for putting on the steam like that."

Larry's cab was standing next to ours. He flung open the door and said, "I'm your man, gentlemen! Take my cab, my horse will get you there all right," and as he shut them in, with a wink towards Jerry, said, "It's against his conscience to go beyond a jog-trot" Then, slashing his tired horse, he set off as hard as he could. Jerry patted me on the neck – "No, Jack, a shilling would not pay for that sort of thing, would it, old boy?"

Although Jerry was determinedly set against hard driving to please careless people, he always went a good fair pace, and was not against putting on the steam, as he said, if only he knew *why*.

I well remember one morning, as we were on the stand waiting for a fare, that a young man, carrying a heavy suitcase, stepped on a piece of orange peel which lay on the sidewalk, and fell down with great force.

Jerry was the first to run and lift him up. He seemed almost stunned, and as they led him into a shop, he walked as if he were in great pain. Jerry of course came back to the stand, but in about ten minutes one of the shopmen called him, so he drew up to the sidewalk.

"Can you take me to the South Eastern Railway?" said

the young man. "This unlucky fall has made me late, I fear, but it is of great importance that I should not miss the twelve o'clock train. I would be most thankful if you could get me there in time, and will gladly pay you an extra fare."

"I'll do my very best," said Jerry heartily, "if you think you are well enough, sir," for he looked dreadfully white and ill.

"I *must* go," said he earnestly. "Please let us lose no time."

The next minute Jerry was on the box, with a cheery chirrup to me, and a twitch of the rein that I well understood.

"Now then, Jack, my boy," said he, "spin along, we'll show them how we can get over the ground, if we only know why."

It is always difficult to drive fast in the city in the middle of the day, when the streets are full of traffic, but we did what could be done. And when a good driver and a good horse, who understand each other, are of one mind, it is wonderful what they can do. I had a very good mouth – that is, I could be guided by the slightest touch of the rein, and that is a great thing in London, among carriages, omnibuses, carts, vans, trucks, cabs, and great wagons creeping along at a walking pace, some going one way, some another, some going slowly, others wanting to pass them and omnibuses stopping short every few minutes to take up a passenger. If you want to get through London fast in the middle of the day, it takes a lot of practice.

Jerry and I were used to it, and no one could beat us at getting through when we were set upon it. I was fast, and bold, and could always trust my driver. Jerry was quick, and patient at the same time, and could trust his horse, which was a great thing too. He very seldom used the whip. I knew by his voice, and his "click click", when he wanted to get on fast, and by the rein where I was to go.

The streets were very full that day, but we got on pretty well as far as the bottom of Cheapside, where there was a block for three or four minutes. The young man put his head out, and said anxiously, "I think I had better get out and walk, I shall never get there if this goes on."

"I'll do all that can be done, sir," said Jerry. "I think we shall be in time. This hold-up cannot last much longer, and your luggage is very heavy for you to carry, sir."

Just then the cart in front of us began to move on, and then we had a good turn. In and out – in and out we went, as fast as horseflesh could do it, and for a wonder had a good clear time on London Bridge, for there was a whole train of cabs and carriages, all going our way at a quick

trot – perhaps wanting to catch that very train; at any rate we whirled into the station with many more, just as the great clock pointed to eight minutes to twelve o'clock.

"Thank God! we are in time," said the young man, "and thank you too and your good horse. You have saved me more than money can ever pay for; take this extra half-crown."

"No, sir, no, thank you all the same. So glad we made the time, sir, but don't stay now, sir, the bell is ringing. Here, porter! take this gentleman's luggage – Dover line – twelve o'clock train – that's it." And without waiting for another word, Jerry wheeled me around to make room for other cabs that were dashing up at the last minute, and drew up on one side until the crush was past.

"So glad!" he said, "so glad! poor young fellow! I wonder what it was that made him so anxious!"

On Jerry's return to the rank, there was a good deal of laughing at him for driving hard to the train for an extra fare, as they said, all against his principles, and they wanted to know how much he had pocketed.

"A good deal more than I generally get," said he, "what he gave me will keep me in little comforts for several days.'

"Go on!" said one.

"He's a humbug," said another, "preaching to us, and then doing the same himself."

"Look here, mates," said Jerry. "The gentleman offered me half-a-crown extra, but I didn't take it; 'twas quite pay enough for me, to see how glad he was to catch that train; and if Jack and I choose to have a quick run now and then, to please ourselves, that's our business and not yours."

"Well," said Larry, "*you'll* never be a rich man."

"Most likely not," said Jerry, "but I don't know that I

shall be the less happy for that. I have heard the commandments read a great many times, and I never noticed that any of them said, 'Thou shalt be rich' – and there are a good many curious things said in the New Testament about rich men, that I think would make me feel rather queer if I was one of them."

"If you ever do get rich," said Governor, "you'll deserve it, Jerry, and you won't find a curse come with your wealth. As for you, Larry, you'll die poor, you spend too much in whipcord."

"Well," said Larry, "what is a fellow to do if his horse won't go without it?"

"You never take the trouble to see if he will go without it. Your whip is always going as if you had the St Vitus' dance in your arm. If it does not wear you out, it wears your horse out. You know you are always changing your horses, and why? Because you never give them any peace or encouragement."

"Well, I have not had good luck," said Larry, "that's what it is."

"And you never will," said the Governor. "Good Luck is rather particular who she rides with, and mostly prefers those who have got common sense and a good heart; at least, that is my experience."

Governor Grant turned around again to his newspaper, and the other men went to their cabs.

36. The Sunday Cab

ONE morning a gentleman walked into the yard.

"Good morning, Mr. Barker," he said. "I would be glad to make some arrangement with you for taking Mrs. Briggs regularly to church on Sunday mornings. We go to the New Church now, and that is rather further than she can walk."

"Thank you, sir," said Jerry, "but I have only taken out a six days' permit and therefore I could not take a fare on a Sunday. It would not be legal."

"Oh!" said the other, "I did not know that. But of course it would be very easy to get one for seven days. I would see that you did not lose by it. The fact is, Mrs. Briggs very much prefers you to drive her."

"I should be glad to oblige the lady, sir, but I had a seven days' permit once, and the work was too hard for me, and for my horses. Year in and year out, not a day's rest, never a Sunday with my wife and children, and never able to go to church, which I always used to do before I took to the driving box. So for the last five years I have only taken a six days' permit, and I find it better altogether."

"Well, of course," replied Mr. Briggs, "it is very proper that every person should have rest, and be able to go to church on Sundays, but I would have thought you would not have minded such a short distance for the horse, and only once a week; you would have all the afternoon and evening for yourself, and we are very good customers, you know."

"Yes, sir, that is true, and I am grateful, and anything that I could do to oblige you, or the lady, I should be proud and happy to do; but I can't give up my Sundays, sir. I read that God made man, and He made horses, and as soon as He had made them, He made a day of rest, and bade that all should rest one day in seven; and I think, sir, He must have known what was good for them, and I am sure it is good for me. I am stronger and healthier altogether, now that I have a day of rest. The horses are fresh too, and do not wear out nearly so fast. The six day drivers all tell me the same. I have more money laid by in the Savings Bank than ever before; and as for the wife and children, sir, they would not go back to the seven days for anything.

"Oh, very well," said the gentleman. "Don't trouble yourself any further, Mr. Barker, I will inquire somewhere else." And he walked away.

"Well," says Jerry to me, "we can't help it, Jack, old boy, we must have our Sundays."

"Polly!" he shouted, "Polly! come here."

"What is it all about, Jerry?"

"Mr. Briggs wants me to take Mrs. Briggs to church every Sunday morning. I say I have only a six days' permit. He says, 'Get a seven days' permit and I'll make it worth your while,' and you know, Polly, they are very good customers to us. Mrs. Briggs often goes out shopping for hours, or making calls, and then she pays down fair like a lady; there's no beating down, as some folks do. And it is easy work for the horses, not like tearing along to catch trains for people that are always a quarter of an hour too late; and if I don't oblige her in this matter, it is very likely we shall lose them altogether. What do you say, little woman?"

"I say, Jerry," said she, speaking very slowly, "I say, if Mrs. Briggs would give you a sovereign every Sunday morning, I would not have you a seven days' cabman again. We have known what it was to have no Sundays; and now we know what it is to call them our own. Thank God, you earn enough to keep us, though it is sometimes hard to manage, but Harry will soon be earning something, and I would rather struggle on harder than we do, than go back to those bad times, when you hardly had a minute to look at your own children, and we never could go to church together, or have a happy, quiet day."

"And that is just what I told Mr. Briggs, my dear," said Jerry. "Don't go and fret yourself, Polly" (for she had begun to cry); "I would not go back to the old times if I earned twice as much, so that is settled, little woman. Now cheer up, and I'll be off again to the stand."

Three weeks after this conversation no order had come from Mrs. Briggs, so there was nothing but taking jobs from the stand. Jerry took it to heart a good deal, for of course the work was harder for horse and man. But Polly would cheer him up and say, "Never mind, Jerry:

Do your best,
And leave the rest,
'Twill all come right,
Some day or night."

It soon became known that Jerry had lost his best customer, and why; most of the men said he was a fool, but two or three took his part.

"If working men don't stick to their Sunday," said Truman, "they'll soon have none left. It is every man's right and every beast's right. By God's law we have a day of rest, and by the law of England we have a day of rest, and I say we ought to hold to the rights these laws give us, and keep them for our children."

"All very well for you religious chaps to talk so," said Larry, "but I'll turn a shilling when I can. I don't believe in religion, for I don't see that your religious people are any better than the rest."

"If they are not better," put in Jerry, "it is because they are *not* religious. You might as well say that laws are not good because some people break them. If a man gives way to his temper, and speaks evil of other people, and does not pay his debts, he is *not* religious. I don't care how much he goes to church. If some men are shams and humbugs, that does not make religion untrue. Real religion is the best and the truest thing in the world, and the only thing that can make a man really happy, or make the world any better."

"If religion was good for anything," said Jones, "it would prevent your religious people from making us work on

Sundays as you know many of them do, and that's why I say religion is nothing but a sham. Why, if it was not for the church and chapel-goers it would be hardly worth while our coming out on a Sunday; but they have their privileges, and I go without. I shall expect them to answer for my soul, if I can't get a chance of saving it."

Several of the men applauded this, until Jerry said:

"That may sound well enough, but it won't do. Every man must look after his own soul; you can't lay it down at another man's door like a foundling, and expect him to take care of it. If you are always sitting on your box waiting for a fare, they will say, 'If we don't take him, some one else will, and he does not want his Sunday.' Of course they don't think it out, or they would see if they never came for a cab, it would be no use your standing there. But people don't always like to get to the bottom of things. If you Sunday drivers would all strike for a day of rest, the thing would be done"

"And what would all the good people do, if they could not get to the preachers they like best?" said Larry.

"It's not for me to lay down plans for other people," said Jerry, "but if they can't walk so far, they can go to what is nearer; and if it rains they can put on their rain-coats as they do on a weekday. If a thing is right, it *can* be done, and if it is wrong, it *can be done without*. A good man will find a way; and that is as true for us cabmen as it is for the church-goers."

37. The Golden Rule

Two or three weeks after this, as we came into the yard in the evening, Polly came running across the road.

"It has all come right, Jerry; Mrs. Briggs sent her servant this afternoon to ask you to take her out to morrow at eleven o'clock. I said, 'Yes, I thought so, but we supposed she employed some one else now.'

" 'Well,' says he, 'the real fact is, master was put out because Mr. Barker refused to come on Sundays, and he has been trying other cabs, but there's something wrong with them all; some drive too fast, and some too slow, and the mistress says there is not one of them so nice as yours, and nothing will suit her but Mr. Barker's cab again.' "

Polly was almost out of breath, and Jerry broke out into a merry laugh.

"All come right some day or night; you were right, my dear. You generally are. Run in and get the supper, and I'll have Jack's harness off in no time."

After this, Mrs. Briggs wanted Jerry's cab quite as often as before, though never on a Sunday. But there came a day when we had Sunday work, and it happened thus.

We had all come home on the Saturday night very tired, and were looking forward to our Sunday rest. On Sunday morning Jerry was cleaning me in the yard when Polly stepped up to him, looking very full of something.

"What is it?" said Jerry.

"Poor Dinah Brown has just heard that her mother is dangerously ill, and that she must go directly if she wishes to see her alive. The place is more than ten miles away, out in the country, and she says if she takes the train she would still have four miles to walk. Weak as she is, and the baby only four weeks old, of course that would be impossible. She wants to know if you would take her in your cab, and she promises to pay you faithfully as soon as she can get the money."

"It's not the money I'm thinking about, but losing our Sunday; the horses are tired, and I am tired too – that's where it pinches."

"It pinches all around for that matter," said Polly, "for it's only half Sunday without you, but you know we should do to other people as we should like them to do to us; and I know very well what I should like if my mother was dying. Jerry, dear, I am sure it won't break the Sabbath, for if pulling a poor beast or donkey out of a pit would not spoil it, I am quite sure taking poor Dinah would not do it."

"Why, Polly, you are as good as the minister! Go and tell Dinah that I'll be ready for her at ten; but stop – just ask butcher Braydon if he would lend me his light trap. I know he never uses it on the Sunday."

Away she went, and soon returned, saying that he could have the trap and welcome.

"All right," said he. "Now put me up a bit of bread and cheese, and I'll be back in the afternoon as soon as I can."

"And I'll have the meat pie ready for an early tea instead of for dinner," said Polly, and away she went.

I was selected for the journey, and at ten o'clock we started, in a light, high-wheeled gig, which ran so easily that after the four-wheeled cab, it seemed like nothing.

It was a fine May day, and as soon as we were out of the town, the sweet air, the smell of the fresh grass, and the soft country roads were as pleasant as they used to be in the old times, and I soon began to feel quite fresh.

Dinah's family lived in a small farmhouse, up a green

lane, close by a meadow, with some fine shady trees: there were two cows feeding in it. A young man asked Jerry to bring his trap into the meadow, and he would tie me up in the cowshed; he wished he had a better stable to offer.

"If your cows would not be offended," said Jerry, "there is nothing my horse would like so well as to have an hour or two in your beautiful meadow".

"Do, and welcome," said the young man. "The best we have is at your service for your kindness to my sister. We shall be having some dinner in an hour, and I hope you'll come in, though with mother so ill, we are all out of sorts in the house."

Jerry thanked him kindly, but said, he wouldn't as he had some dinner with him.

When my harness was taken off, I did not know what I should do first – eat the grass, or roll over on my back, or lie down and rest, or have a gallop across the meadow out of sheer spirits at being free – and I did all by turns. Jerry seemed to be quite as happy as I was; he sat down by a bank under a shady tree and listened to the birds, then he sang himself, and read out of the little brown book he was so fond of, then wandered around the meadow and down by a little brook, where he picked the flowers and the hawthorn, and tied them up with long sprays of ivy. Then he gave me a good feed of oats which he had brought with him. But the time seemed all too short – I had not been in a field since I left poor Ginger at Earlshall.

We came home gently, and Jerry said, "Well, Polly, I have not lost my Sunday after all, for the birds were singing hymns in every bush, and I joined in the service – and as for Jack, he was like a young colt."

He handed Dolly the flowers and she jumped for joy.

176

38. Dolly and a Real Gentleman

THE winter came in early, very cold and wet. There was snow or sleet or rain almost every day for weeks, changing only for keen driving winds, or sharp frosts. We horses all felt it very much. When it is a dry cold, a couple of good thick rugs will keep the warmth in us; but in soaking rain, they soon get wet through and are no good. Some of the drivers had a waterproof cover to throw over, which was a fine thing; but some of the men were so poor that they could not protect either themselves or their horses, and many of them suffered very much that winter. When we horses had worked half the day we went to our dry stables, and could rest; while they had to sit on their boxes, sometimes staying out as late as one or two o'clock in the morning, if they had a party to wait for.

When the streets were slippery with frost or snow, that was the worst of all for us horses. One mile of such going with a weight to draw, and no firm footing, would take more out of us than four on a good road; every nerve and muscle of our bodies was straining to keep our balance, and added to this, the fear of falling was more exhausting than anything else. If the roads were very bad indeed, our shoes were roughed, but that made us feel nervous as first.

When the weather was very bad, many of the men would go and sit in the tavern close by, and get some one to watch for them; but they often lost a fare in that way, and as Jerry said, could not be there without spending money. He never went to the "Rising Sun"; there was a coffee shop near, where he went now and then – or he bought hot coffee and pies from an old man near our rank. It was his opinion that spirits and beer made a man colder afterwards, and that dry clothes, good food, cheerfulness, and a comfortable wife at home, were the best things to keep a cabman warm. Polly always supplied him with something to eat when he could not get home, and sometimes he would see little Dolly peeping from the corner of the street, to see if her father was on the stand. If she saw him, she would run off at full speed and soon come back with something in a tin or basket – some hot soup or pudding that Polly had ready. It was wonderful how such a little thing could get safely across the street, often thronged with horses and carriages; but she was a brave little girl, and felt it a privilege.

One cold windy day, Dolly had brought Jerry a bowl of something hot, and was standing by him while he ate it. He had scarcely begun, when a gentleman waved to him. Jerry touched his hat in return, gave the bowl to Dolly, and was taking off my cloth, when the gentleman, hastening up, cried out, "No, no, finish your soup, my friend. I can wait until you have finished, and seen your little girl across the road." So saying, he seated himself in the cab. Jerry thanked him kindly, and came back to Dolly.

"That's a real gentleman, Dolly; he has got time for the comfort of a poor cabman and a little girl."

Jerry finished his soup, saw the child across, and then drove off. Several times after that, the same gentleman took our cab. Sometimes he came up and patted me, saying in his quiet, pleasant way, "This horse has got a good master, and he deserves it." It was a very rare thing for any one to notice the horse that had been working for him. I have known ladies do it now and then, and this gentleman, and one or two others.

This gentleman was not young, and there was a forward stoop in his shoulders as if he was always going towards something. His lips were thin, and close shut, though they had a very pleasant smile. His eye was keen, and there was something in his jaw and the motion of his head that made one think he was very determined in anything he set about. His voice was pleasant and kind.

One day, he and another gentleman took our cab; they stopped at a shop and while his friend went in, he stood at the door. A little ahead of us on the other side of the street, a cart with two very fine horses was standing before some wine vaults. The driver was not with them, and I cannot tell how long they had been standing, but they seemed to think they had waited long enough, and began to move off. Before they had gone far, the driver came running out and caught them. He seemed furious at their having moved, and whipped them brutally – even beating them about the head. Our gentleman saw it all and stepping quickly across the street, said:

"If you don't stop that immediately, I'll have you summoned for brutal conduct."

The man, who had clearly been drinking, swore at him, but he left off knocking the horses about, and, taking the reins, got into his cart. Meanwhile our friend had quietly taken a notebook from his pocket, and, looking at the name and address on the cart, he wrote it down.

"What do you want with that?" growled the driver, as he cracked his whip and was moving on. A nod, and a grim smile, was the only answer he got.

On returning to the cab, our friend was joined by his companion, who said laughingly, "I should have thought, Wright, you had enough business of your own to look after, without troubling yourself about other people's horses and servants."

"Do you know why this world is as bad as it is?" asked our friend.

"No," said the other.

"Then I'll tell you. It is because people think *only* about their own business, and won't trouble themselves to stand up for the oppressed. I never see a wicked thing like this without doing what I can, and many a master has thanked me for letting him know how his horses have been used."

"I wish there were more gentlemen like you, sir," said Jerry, "for we are badly in need of them in this city."

After this we continued our journey, and as they got out of the cab, our friend was saying, "If we see cruelty or wrong that we have the power to stop, and do nothing, we make ourselves sharers in the guilt."

39. Seedy Sam

I SHOULD say, that for a cab horse I was very well off indeed; my driver was my owner, and it was his interest to treat me well, and not overwork me, even had he not been so good a man as he was. But there were a great many horses which belonged to the large cab-owners, who let them out to their drivers for so much money a day. As the horses did not belong to these men, the only thing they thought of was how to get their money out of them: first, to pay the master, and then to provide for their own living; and a dreadful time some of these horses had of it. It was often talked over on the stand, and the Governor, who was a kindhearted man, and fond of horses, would sometimes speak up if one came in very tired or ill-used.

One day, a shabby, miserable-looking driver, who went by the name of "Seedy Sam", brought in his horse looking dreadfully tired and the Governor said;

"You and your horse look more fit for the police station than for this rank."

The man flung his tattered rug over the horse, turned upon the Governor, and said, in a desperate voice:

"The police ought to see about the masters who charge us so much, or the fares that are fixed so low. Many of us have to pay eighteen shillings a day for the use of a cab and two horses, and must make that up before we earn a penny for ourselves. If the horses don't work we must starve. I've six children, and only one earns anything. I am on the stand fourteen or sixteen hours a day, and I haven't had a Sunday these twelve weeks – you know Skinner never gives a day if he can help it; and if I don't work hard, tell me who does! I want a warm coat but with so many to feed, how can a man get them?"

Some of the other drivers stood around nodding their heads, and saying he was right. The man went on:

"You who have your own horses and cabs, or drive for good masters, have a chance of getting on, and a chance of doing right. I haven't. We can't charge more than sixpence a mile after the first, within the four mile radius. This very morning I had to go a clear six miles and only took three shillings. I could not get a return fare, and had to come all the way back; there's twelve miles for the horse and three shillings for me. After that I had a three mile fare, and there were bags and boxes enough to have brought in a good many twopences if they had been put outside. But you know what people do; all that could be piled up inside on the front seat were put in, and three heavy boxes went on the top. That was sixpence, and the fare one and sixpence. Then I got a return for a shilling. Now that makes eighteen miles for the horse and six shillings for me; there's three shillings still for that horse to earn, and nine shillings for the afternoon horse before I touch a penny. Of course it is not always as bad as that, but you know it often is, and I say its a mockery to tell a man that he must not overwork his horse, for when a beast is exhausted, there's nothing but the whip that will keep his legs going. You can't help yourself – you must put your wife and children before the horse – the masters must see to that, we can't. Never a day's rest, never a quiet hour with the wife and children. I often feel like an old man, though I'm forty-five. You know how quick some of the gentry are to suspect us of cheating and overcharging. They stand with their purses in their hands, counting it over to a penny, and looking at us as if we were pickpockets. I wish some of 'em had got to sit on my box sixteen hours a day in all weathers, and get a living out of it, and eighteen shillings besides; they would not be so uncommon particular never to give us a sixpence over, or to cram all the luggage inside. Of course, some of 'em tip us pretty handsome now and then, or else we could not live, but you can't *depend* upon that."

The others agreed, and one said, "It is hard, and if a man sometimes does what is wrong, it is no wonder; and if he takes a dram too much, who's to blame him?"

Jerry had taken no part in this conversation, but I never saw him look so sad before. The Governor took his handkerchief out of his hat, and wiped his forehead.

"You've beaten me, Sam," he said, "for it's all true; it was the look in that horse's eye that came over me. It is hard lines for man and for beast, and who's to mend it I don't know. But anyway you might tell the poor beast that you were sorry to take it out of him in that way. Sometimes a kind word is all we can give 'em, poor brutes."

A week later a new man came on the stand with Sam's cab.

"Hullo!" said one. "What's up with Seedy Sam?"

"He's ill," said the man. "He was taken sick last night in the yard, and could scarcely crawl home. His wife sent a boy this morning to say he was in a high fever and could not get up; so I'm here instead."

The next morning the same man came again.

"How is Sam?" inquired the Governor.

"He's gone," said the man.

"What, gone? You don't mean to say he's dead?"

"Just snuffed out," said the other. "He died at four o'clock this morning. All yesterday he was raving – raving about Skinner, and having no Sundays. 'I never had a Sunday's rest.' Those were his last words."

40. Poor Ginger

ONE day, while our cab and many others were waiting outside one of the Parks, where a band was playing, a shabby old cab drove up beside ours. The horse was an old worn-out chestnut, with an ill-kept coat, and bones that showed plainly through it. The knees knuckled over, and the forelegs were very unsteady. I had been eating some hay, and the wind rolled a little lock of it that way, and the poor creature put out her long thin neck and picked it up, and then turned around and looked about for more. There was a hopeless look in the dull eye that I could not help noticing, and then, as I was thinking where I had seen that horse before, she looked full at me and said, "Black Beauty, is that you?"

It was Ginger! but how changed! Her beautifully arched and glossy neck was now straight and lank and fallen in, her clean straight legs and delicate fetlocks were swelled; her joints were grown out of shape with hard work; her face – that was once so full of spirit – was now full of suffering, and I could tell by the heaving of her sides, and her frequent cough, how bad her wind was.

It was a sad tale that she had to tell. After a twelve-months' rest at Earlshall, she was considered to be fit for work again, and was sold to a gentleman. For a little while she got on very well, but after a longer gallop than usual the old strain returned, and after being rested and doctered she was again sold. In this way she changed hands several times, but always getting lower down.

"And so at last," said she "I was bought by a man who keeps a number of cabs and horses, and lets them out. You look well off, and I am glad of it, but I could not tell you what my life has been. When they found out my weakness, they said I was not worth what they gave for me, and that I must go into one of the low cabs, and just be used up. That is what they are doing, whipping and working me with never one thought of what I suffer. They paid for me, and must get it out of me, they say. The man who hires me pays a large sum of money to the owner every day, and so he has to get it out of me too; and so it's all the week around with never a Sunday rest."

I said, "You used to stand up for yourself if you were ill-used."

"Ah!" she said, "I did once, but it's no use; men are stronger, and if they are cruel and have no feeling, there is nothing that we can do, but just bear it, on and on to the end. I wish the end would come, I wish I was dead. I have seen dead horses, and I am sure they do not suffer pain. I wish I may drop down dead at my work, and not be sent off to the slaughterhouse."

I was very much troubled, but I could say nothing to comfort her. I think she was pleased to see me, for she said, "You are the only friend I ever had."

Just then her driver came up, and with a tug at her mouth backed her out of the line and drove off, leaving me very sad indeed.

A short time after this a cart with a dead horse in it passed our cab stand. The head hung out of the cart tail, the lifeless tongue was slowly dripping with blood; and the sunken eyes! but I can't speak of them, the sight was too dreadful. It was a chestnut horse with a long thin neck. I saw a white streak down the forehead. I believe it was Ginger. I hoped it was, for then her troubles would be over. Oh! if men were more merciful, they would shoot us before we came to such misery.

41. The Butcher

I saw a great deal of trouble among the horses in London, and much of it that might have been prevented by a little common sense. We horses do not mind hard work if we are treated reasonably, and I am sure there are many driven by quite poor men who have a happier life than I had when I used to go in the Countess of W—'s carriage.

It often went to my heart to see how the little ponies were used, straining along with heavy loads, or staggering under heavy blows from some cruel boy. Once I saw a little gray pony with a thick mane and a pretty head, and so much like Merrylegs, that if I had not been in harness, I would have neighed to him. He was doing his best to pull a heavy cart, while a great rough boy was cutting him under the belly with his whip, and chucking cruelly at his little mouth. Could it be Merrylegs? It was just like him; but then Mr. Blomefield was never to sell him, and I do not think he would; but this might have been quite as good a little fellow and had as happy a place when he was young.

I often noticed the great speed at which butchers' horses were made to go, though I did not know why it was so, until one day when we had to wait some time in "St. John's Wood". There was a butcher's shop next door, and, as we were standing, a butcher's cart came dashing up at a great pace. The horse was hot and much exhausted. He hung his head down, while his heaving sides and trembling legs showed how hard he had been driven. The lad jumped out of the cart and was getting the basket, when the master came out of the shop much displeased. After looking at the horse, he turned angrily to the lad:

"How many times must I tell you not to drive in this way? You ruined the last horse and broke his wind, and you are going to ruin this in the same way. If you were not my own son, I would dismiss you on the spot. It is a disgrace to have a horse brought to the shop in a condition like that. You are liable to be taken up by the police for such driving, and if you are, you need not look to me for bail, for I have spoken to you until I am tired; you must look out for yourself."

During this speech, the boy had stood by, sullen and dogged, but when his father ceased, he broke out angrily. It wasn't his fault, and he wouldn't take the blame, he was only going by orders all the time.

"You always say, 'Now be quick; now look sharp!' and when I got to the houses, one wanted a leg of mutton for an early dinner, and I must be back with it in a quarter of an hour. Another cook had forgotten to order the beef, so I must go and collect it and be back in no time, or the mistress will scold, and the housekeeper says they have company coming unexpectedly and must have some chops sent up immediately, and the lady at No. 4, in the Crescent, *never* orders her dinner until the meat comes in for lunch, and it's nothing but hurry, hurry, all the time. If the gentry would think of what they want, and order their meat the day before, there need not be this blowup!"

"I wish to goodness they would," said the butcher; "it would save me a great amount of trouble, and I could suit my customers much better if I knew beforehand. But what's the use of talking. Who ever thinks of a butcher's convenience, or a butcher's horse? Now then, take him in, and look after him well. Mind, he does not go out again today, and if anything else is wanted, you must carry it yourself in the basket."

But all boys are not cruel. I have seen some as fond of their pony or donkey as if it had been a pet dog, and the little creatures have worked away as cheerfully and willingly for their young drivers as I worked for Jerry. It may be hard work sometimes, but a friend's hand and voice make it easy.

There was a young barrowboy who came up our street with greens and potatoes; he had an old pony, not very handsome, but the cheerfullest and pluckiest little thing I ever saw, and to see how fond those two were of each other, was a treat. The pony followed his master like a dog, and when he got into his cart, would trot off without a whip or a word, and rattle down the street as merrily as if he had come out of the Queen's stables. Jerry liked the boy, and called him "Prince Charlie", for he said he would make a king of drivers some day.

There was an old man, too, who used to come up our street with a little coal cart. He wore a coalheaver's hat, and looked rough and black. He and his old horse used to plod together along the street, like two good partners who understood each other; the horse would stop of his own accord, at the doors where they took coal of him; he used to keep one ear bent toward his master. The old man's cry could be heard up the street long before he came near. I never knew what he said, but the children called him "Old Ba-a-ar Hoo", for it sounded like that. Polly got her coal from him, and was very friendly, and Jerry said it was a comfort to think how happy an old horse *might* be in even a poor place.

42. The Election

As we came into the yard one afternoon, Polly came out. "Jerry! I've had Mr. B— here asking about your vote, and he wants to hire your cab for the election; he will call for an answer."

"Well, Polly, you may say that my cab will be otherwise engaged; I would not like to have it pasted over with their great bills, and as for having Jack and Captain race to the public houses to bring up half-drunken voters, why I think it would be an insult to the horses. No, I shan't do it."

"I suppose you'll vote for the gentleman? He said he was of your politics."

"So he is in some things, but I shall not vote for him, Polly; you know what his trade is?"

"Yes."

"Well, a man who gets rich by that trade, may be all very well in some ways, but he is blind as to what working men want; I could not in my conscience help him to make the laws."

On the morning before the election, Jerry was putting me into the shafts, when Dolly came into the yard sobbing and crying, with her little blue frock and white pinafore spattered all over with mud.

"Why, Dolly, what is the matter?"

"Those naughty boys," she sobbed, "have thrown the dirt all over me."

"They won't insult my sister again," said Harry, who ran in looking very angry. "I have given them a thrashing they will remember; a set of cowardly, rascally, orange blackguards!"

Jerry kissed the child and said, "Run in to mother, my pet, and tell her I think you had better stay at home today and help her."

Then turning gravely to Harry:

"My boy, I hope you will always defend your sister, and give anybody who insults her a good thrashing – that is as it should; but mind, I won't have any election blackguarding on my premises. There are as many blue blackguards as there are orange, and as many white as there are purple, or any other badge, and I won't have any of my family mixed up with it. Even women and children are ready to quarrel for the sake of a badge, and not one in ten of them knows what it is about."

"Why, father, I thought blue was for Liberty."

"My boy, Liberty does not come from badges; they only show party, and all the liberty you can get out of them is liberty to get drunk at other people's expense, liberty to ride to the poll in a dirty old cab, liberty to abuse any one

that does not wear your badge, and to shout yourself hoarse at what you only half understand – that's your liberty!"

"Oh, father, you are laughing."

"No, Harry, I am serious, and I am ashamed to see how men go on that ought to know better. An election is a very serious thing – at least it ought to be; and every man ought to vote according to his conscience, and let other people do the same."

43. A Friend in Need

AT last came the election day and plenty of work for us.
First came a stout puffy gentleman with a carpet bag. He
wanted to go to Bishopsgate Station. Then we took somebody to the Regent's Park; and next we were wanted in
a side street where a timid old lady was waiting to be
taken to the bank: there we had to wait to take her back
again – and just as we had set her down, a red-faced
gentleman came running up out of breath, and before
Jerry could get down, he had opened the door, popped
himself in, and called out, "Bow Street Police Station,
quick!" So off we went with him and when after another
turn or two we came back, there was no other cab on the
stand. Jerry put on my nose bag, for as he said, "We must
eat when we can on such days as these, so munch away,
Jack, and make the best of your time, old boy."

I found I had a good feed of crushed oats wetted up
with a little bran, this would be a treat any day, but was
specially refreshing then. Jerry was so thoughtful and
kind – what horse would not do his best for such a master? Then he took out one of Polly's meat pies, and standing near me, he began to eat it. The streets were very full,
and the cabs with the Candidates' markings on them were
dashing about through the crowd as if life and limb were
of no consequence. We saw a man and a woman knocked
down that day. The horses were having a bad time of it,
poor things! but the voters inside thought nothing of
that, many of them were drunk, and yelling out of the
cab windows if their own party came by. It was the first
election I had seen, and I don't want to be in another,
although I have heard things are better now.

Jerry and I had not eaten many mouthfuls before a poor young woman, carrying a heavy child, came along the street. She seemed lost and bewildered. Presently she made her way up to Jerry, and asked the way to St Thomas' Hospital. She had come from the country that morning, she said, in a market cart; she did not know about the election and was quite a stranger in London. She had got an order for the Hospital for her little boy. The child was crying feebly.

"Poor little fellow!" she said. "He suffers a lot of pain; he is four years old and can't walk; but the doctor said if I could get him into the Hospital, he might get well. Please, how far is it? and which way?"

"Why, missis," said Jerry, "you can't get there walking through crowds like this! It's three miles away, and that child is heavy."

"Yes, he is, but I am strong, thank God, and I think I can manage somehow. Please tell me the way."

"You can't do it," said Jerry. "You might be knocked down and the child be run over. Now, look here, just get into this cab, and I'll drive you safe to the hospital; don't you see the rain is starting?"

"No, sir, no, I can't do that, thank you. I have only just money enough to get back with. Please tell me the way."

"Look here, missis," said Jerry, "I've got a wife and children at home, and I know a father's feelings. Now get you into that cab, and I'll take you there for nothing; I'd be ashamed of myself to let a woman and a sick child run a risk like that."

"Heaven bless you!" said the woman, and burst into tears.

"There, there, cheer up, my dear, I'll soon take you there. Come, let me put you inside.'

As Jerry went to open the door, two men, with badges in their hats and buttonholes, ran up, calling out, "Cab!"

"Engaged," cried Jerry; but one of the men, pushing past the woman, sprang into the cab, followed by the other. Jerry looked as stern as a policeman: "This cab is already engaged, gentlemen, by that lady."

"She can wait," said one of them, "our business is very important. Besides we were in first, it is our right, and we shall stay in."

Jerry smiled and shut the door upon them. "All right, gentlemen, stay in as long as it suits you. I can wait while you rest yourselves." Turning his back upon them, he walked up to the young woman, who was standing near me. "They'll soon be gone," he said, laughing, "so don't trouble yourself, my dear."

And they soon were gone, for when they understood that Jerry meant to be firm, they got out, calling him all sorts of bad names, and blustering about his number, and getting a summons. After this little delay we were soon on our way to the hospital, going as much as possible through side streets. Jerry helped the young woman out and rang the great bell.

"Thank you a thousand times," she said. "I could never have got here alone."

"You're very welcome, and I hope the child will soon be better."

He watched her go in at the door. Then he patted my neck, which was always his way when anything pleased him.

It was raining hard, and just as we were leaving the hospital the porter called out, "Cab!" We stopped, and a lady came down the steps. Jerry seemed to know her at once; she put back her veil and said, "Jeremiah Barker!

is it you? I am very glad to find you here. You are just the friend I want, for it is very difficult to get a cab in this part of London today."

"I am right glad I happened to be here; where may I take you to, ma'am?"

"To Paddington Station, and then if we are in good time, you shall tell me all about Mary and the children."

We got to the station in good time, and the lady stood a good while talking to Jerry. I found she had been Polly's mistress, and after many inquiries about her, she said:

"How do you find the cab work suits you in winter? I know Mary was rather anxious about you last year."

"Yes, ma'am, she was; I had a bad cough that stayed with me into the warm weather, and when I am kept out late, she worries herself a good deal. You see, ma'am, it is all hours and all weathers, and that does try a man's constitution; but I am getting on pretty well, and I would feel quite lost if I had not horses to look after. I was brought up to it, and I am afraid I should not do so well at anything else."

"Well, Barker," she said, "it seems a great pity that you should seriously risk your health in this work. There are many places where good drivers or good grooms are wanted; and if ever you think you ought to give up this cab work, let me know." Then, sending some kind messages to Mary, she put something into his hand, saying, "There is five shillings each for the two children; Mary will know how to spend it."

Jerry thanked her and seemed much pleased. Turning out of the station, we at last reached home, and I, at least, was tired.

44. Old Captain and his Successor

CAPTAIN and I were great friends, but at last the day came when he had to leave his home and go down the hill. I was not there, but I heard all about it.

He and Jerry had taken a party to London Bridge station, and were coming back, somewhere between the Bridge and the Monument, when Jerry saw a brewer's dray coming along, drawn by two powerful horses. The drayman was lashing his horses with his heavy whip. The next moment they dashed up against our cab; both the wheels were torn off, and the cab was thrown over. Captain was dragged down, the shafts splintered, and one of them ran into his side. Jerry too was thrown, but was only bruised; nobody could tell how he escaped, he called it a miracle. Poor Captain was found to be very much cut and knocked about. Jerry led him home gently, and a sad sight it was to see the blood soaking into his white coat, and dropping from his side and shoulder. The drayman was proved to be very drunk, and was fined, and the brewer had to pay damages to Jerry; but there was no one to pay damages to poor Captain.

The farrier and Jerry did the best they could to ease his pain, and make him comfortable. The fly had to be mended, and for several days I did not go out, and Jerry earned nothing. The first time we went to the stand after the accident, the Governor came up to hear how Captain was.

"He'll never get over it," said Jerry. "At least not for my work, so the farrier said this morning. He says he may do for carting, and that sort of work. It has put me out very much. Carting indeed! I've seen what horses come to at

that work around London. I only wish all the drunkards could be put in a lunatic asylum, instead of being allowed to run foul of sober people. If they would break their *own* bones, and smash their *own* carts, and lame their *own* horses, that would be their own affair. But it seems to me that the innocent always suffer; and then they talk about compensation! There's all the trouble, and vexation, and loss of time, besides losing a good horse that's like an old friend – it's nonsense talking of compensation! If there's one devil that I would like to see in the bottomless pit more than another, it's the drink devil."

"I say, Jerry," said the Governor, "you are treading pretty hard on my toes, you know. I'm not as good as you are."

"Well," said Jerry, "why don't you stop it, Governor? You are too good a man to be the slave of such a thing."

"I'm a great fool, Jerry but I tried once for two days, and I thought I would die. How did you do?"

"I had hard work at it for several weeks. You see, I found that I was not my own master, and that when the craving came on, it was hard work to say 'no'. I determined to beat the drink but it was a struggle, and I needed all the help I could get, for until I tried to break the habit, I did not know how strong it was. Polly took pains that I should have good food, and when the craving came on, I used to get a cup of coffee, or some peppermint, or read a bit in my book, and that was a help to me. But thanks be to God, and my dear wife, my chains were broken, and now for ten years I have not tasted a drop, and never wish for it."

"I've a great mind to try it," said Grant, "for it's a poor thing not to be one's own master."

"Do, Governor, do, you'll never repent it. And what a

help it would be to some of the poor fellows in our rank if they saw you do without it. I know there's two or three would like to keep out of that tavern if they could."

At first Captain seemed to do well, but he was a very old horse, and it was only his wonderful constitution, and Jerry's care, that had kept him up at the cab work so long; now he broke down. The farrier said he might improve enough to sell for a few pounds, but Jerry said, no! a few pounds got by selling a good old servant into hard work, and misery, would sour all the rest of his money, and he thought the kindest thing he could do for the fine old fellow would be to shoot him; for he did not know where to find a kind master for the rest of his days.

The day after this was decided, Harry took me to the forge for some new shoes. When I returned, Captain was gone. The family and I all felt it very much.

Jerry had now to look out for another horse, and he soon heard of one through an acquaintance who was under-groom in a nobleman's stables. He was a valuable young horse, but he had run away, smashed into another carriage, flung his lordship out, and so cut and blemished himself that he was no longer fit for a gentleman's stables, and the coachman had orders to look around, and sell him as well as he could.

"I can do with high spirits," said Jerry, "if a horse is not vicious or hard-mouthed."

"There is not a bit of vice in him," said the man. "His mouth is very tender, and I think myself that was the cause of the accident. You see, he had just been clipped, and the weather was bad, and he had not had exercise enough, and when he did go out, he was as full of spring as a balloon. The coachman had him harnessed in as tight and strong as he could, with the martingale, and the bearing rein, a very sharp curb, and the reins put in at the bottom bar; it is my belief that it made the horse mad, being tender in the mouth and so full of spirit."

"Likely enough. I'll come and see him," said Jerry.

The next day, Hotspur – that was his name – came home. He was a fine brown horse, without a white hair in him, as tall as Captain, with a very handsome head, and only five years old. I gave him a friendly greeting by way of good fellowship, but did not ask him any questions. The first night he was very restless; instead of lying down, he kept jerking his halter rope up and down through the ring, and knocking the block about against the manger so that I could not sleep. However, the next day, after five or six hours in the cab, he came in quiet and sensible. Jerry patted and talked to him a good deal, and very soon they understood each other, and Jerry said that with an easy bit, and plenty of work, he would be as gentle as a lamb, and that it was an ill wind that blew nobody good, for if his lordship had lost a hundred guinea thoroughbred, the cabman had gained a good horse with all his strength in him.

Hotspur thought it a great come down to be a cab-horse, and was disgusted at standing in the rank, but he confessed to me at the end of the week that an easy mouth, and a free hand, made up for a great deal, and after all, the work was not so degrading as having one's head and tail fastened to each other at the saddle. In fact, he settled in well, and Jerry liked him very much.

45. Jerry's New Year

CHRISTMAS and New Year are very merry times for some people; but for cabmen and cabmen's horses it is no holiday, though it may be a harvest. There are so many parties that the work is hard and often late. Sometimes driver and horse have to wait for hours in the rain or frost, shivering with cold, while the merry people within are dancing away to the music. I wonder if the beautiful ladies ever think of the weary cabman waiting on his box, and his patient beast standing until his legs get stiff with cold.

I now had most of the evening work, as I was well accustomed to standing, and Jerry was also more afraid of Hotspur taking cold. We had a great deal of late work in the Christmas week, and Jerry's cough was bad; but however late we were, Polly sat up for him, and came out with the lantern to meet him, looking anxious and troubled.

On the evening of the New Year, we had to take two gentlemen to a house in the West End. We set them down at nine o'clock and were told to come again at eleven. "But," said one of them, "as it is a card party, you may have to wait a few minutes, but don't be late."

As the clock struck eleven we were at the door, for Jerry was always punctual. The clock chimed the quarters – one, two, three, and then struck twelve, but the door did not open.

The wind had been very changeable, with squalls of rain during the day, but now it turned into a sharp driving sleet. It was very cold, and there was no shelter. Jerry got off his box and came and pulled one of my cloths a little more over my neck. Then he took a turn or two up and down, stamping his feet. Then he began to beat his arms, but that set him off coughing, so he opened the cab door and sat at the bottom with his feet on the pavement, and was a little sheltered. Still the clock chimed the quarters, and no one came. At half past twelve, he rang the bell and asked the servant if he would be wanted that night.

"Oh! yes," said the man, "you must not go, it will soon be over." And again Jerry sat down, but his voice was so hoarse I could hardly hear him.

At a quarter past one the door opened, and the two gentlemen came out. They got into the cab without a word, and told Jerry where to drive, nearly two miles away. My legs were numb with cold, and I thought I would stumble. When the men got out, they never said they were sorry to have kept us waiting so long, but were angry at the charge. As Jerry never charged more than was his due, so he never took less, and they had to pay for the two hours and a quarter waiting; but it was hard-earned money to Jerry.

At last we got home. He could hardly speak, and his cough was dreadful. Polly asked no questions, but opened the door and held the lantern for him.

"Can't I do something?" she said.

"Yes, get Jack something warm, and then boil me some gruel."

This was said in a hoarse whisper. He could hardly get his breath, but he gave me a rubdown as usual, and even went up into the hayloft for an extra bundle of straw for my bed. Polly brought me a warm mash that made me comfortable, and then they locked the door.

It was late the next morning before any one came, and then it was only Harry. He cleaned us and fed us, and swept out the stalls, then he put the straw back again as if it was Sunday. He was very quiet, and neither whistled nor sang. At noon he came again, and gave us our food and water; this time Dolly came with him; she was crying, and I could gather from what they said that Jerry was dangerously ill, and the doctor said it was a bad case. So two days passed. We only saw Harry and sometimes Dolly. I think she came for company, for Polly was always with Jerry, and he had to be kept very quiet.

On the third day, while Harry was in the stable, a tap came at the door, and Governor Grant came in.

"I wouldn't go to the house, my boy," he said, "but I want to know how your father is."

"He is very bad," said Harry, "they call it 'bronchitis'; the doctor thinks it will turn one way or another tonight."

"That's bad, very bad!" said Grant, shaking his head; "I know two men who died of that last week; but while there's life, there's hope."

"Yes," said Harry, quickly, "and the doctor said that father had a better chance than most men, because he didn't drink. He said yesterday the fever was so high that if father had been a drinking man, it would have burned him up like a piece of paper; but I believe he thinks he will get over it. Don't you think he will, Mr. Grant?"

"If there's any rule that good men should get over these things, I am sure he will, my boy; he's the best man I know. I'll look in early tomorrow."

Early next morning he was there.

"Well?" said he.

"Father is better," said Harry. "Mother hopes he will get over it."

"Thank God!" said the Governor, "and now you must keep him warm, and keep his mind easy. And that brings me to the horses: Jack will be all the better for a week or two 's rest in a warm stable, and you can easily take him a turn up and down the street to stretch his legs. But this young one, if he does not get work, he will soon be all up on end, as you may say, and will be rather too much for you; and when he does go out, there'll be an accident."

"It is like that now," said Harry. "I have kept him short of oats, but he's so full of spirit I don't know what to do with him."

"Just so," said Grant. "Now look here, will you tell your mother that, if she is agreeable, I will come for him every day until something is arranged, and take him for a good spell of work, and whatever he earns I'll bring your mother half of it, and that will help with the horses' feed. Your father is in a good club, I know, but that won't keep the horses, and they'll be eating their heads off all this time. I'll come at noon and hear what she says." And without waiting for Harry's thanks, he was gone.

At noon he saw Polly, and then he harnessed Hotspur and took him out.

For a week or more he came for Hotspur, and when Harry thanked him he laughed it off, saying it was all good luck for him, for his horses were wanting a little rest which they would not otherwise have had.

Jerry grew better, steadily, but the doctor said that he must never go back to the cab work again if he wished to be an old man. The children had many consultations together about what father and mother would do, and how they could help to earn money.

One afternoon, while Harry was sponging off the mud from Hostpur's body and legs, Dolly came in, looking very full of something.

"Who lives at Fairstowe, Harry? Mother has got a letter from Fairstowe; she seemed so glad, and ran up-stairs to father with it."

"Don't you know? Mrs. Fowler – mother's old mistress, you know – the lady that father met last summer, who sent you and me five shillings each."

"Oh! Mrs. Fowler; of course. I wonder what she is writing to mother about."

"Mother wrote to her last week," said Harry. "You know, she told father if ever he gave up the cab work, she would like to know. I wonder what she says. Run in and see, Dolly."

Harry scrubbed away at Hotspur with a huish! huish! like any old ostler.

In a few minutes Dolly came dancing into the stable.

"Oh! Harry, there never was anything so beautiful; Mrs. Fowler says we are all to go and live near her. There is a new cottage that will just suit us, with a garden, and a henhouse, and apple trees, and everything! and her coachman is going away in the spring, and then she will want father in his place; and there are good families near where you can get a place in the garden, or the stable, or as a page boy; and there's a good school for me; and mother is laughing and crying by turns, and father does look *so* happy!"

"That's uncommon jolly," said Harry, "and just the right thing, I should say. It will suit father and mother both, but I don't intend to be a page boy with tight clothes and rows of buttons. I'll be a groom or a gardener."

It was quickly settled that as soon as Jerry was well enough they should move to the country, and that the cab and horses should be sold as soon as possible.

This was heavy news for me, for I was not young now, and could not look for any improvement in my condition. Since I left Birtwick I had never been so happy as with my dear master, Jerry; but three years of cab work, even under the best conditions, will tell on one's strength, and I felt that I was not the horse that I had been.

Grant said at once that he would take Hotspur – and there were men on the stand who would have bought me; but Jerry said I should not go to cab work again with just anybody, and the Governor promised to find a place for me where I should be comfortable.

The day came for going away. Jerry had not been allowed to go out yet, and I never saw him after that New Year's Eve. Polly came with the children to bid me goodbye. "Poor old Jack! dear old Jack! I wish we could take you with us," she said, and then, laying her hand on my mane, she put her face close to my neck and kissed me. Dolly was crying and kissed me too. Harry stroked me a great deal, but said nothing, only he seemed very sad, and so I was led away to my new place.

46. Jakes and the Lady

I WAS sold to a baker whom Jerry knew, and with whom he thought I should have good food and fair work. In the first he was quite right, and if my master had always been on the premises, I do not think I should have been over-loaded; but there was a foreman who was always hurrying and driving every one, and frequently when I had quite a full load, he would order something else to be taken on. My driver, whose name was Jakes, often said it was more than I ought to take, but the other took no notice.

Jakes always had the bearing rein up, which prevented me from drawing easily, and by the time I had been there three or four months, I found the work telling very much on my strength.

One day, I was loaded more than usual, and part of the road was a steep hill. I used all my strength, but I could not get on, and was continually obliged to stop. This did not please my driver, and he laid his whip on badly. "Get on, you lazy fellow," he said, "or I'll make you."

Again I started the heavy load, and struggled on a few yards. Again the whip came down, and again I struggled forward. The pain of that great cart whip was sharp, but my mind was hurt quite as much as my poor sides. To be punished and abused when I was doing my very best was so hard, it took the heart out of me. A third time he was whipping me cruelly, when a lady stepped quickly up to him, and said in a sweet, earnest voice.

"Please do not whip your good horse any more! The road is very steep and I am sure he is doing his best."

"If doing his best won't get this load up, he must do something more than his best, ma'am," said Jakes.

"But is it not a very heavy load?" she said.

"Yes, too heavy," he said. "But that's not my fault; the foreman came just as we were starting, and would have three hundredweight more put on to save him trouble, and I must get on with it as well as I can."

He was raising the whip again, when the lady said:

"I think I can help you if you will let me. You see, you do not give him a fair chance; he cannot use all his power with his head held back as it is with that bearing rein. If you would take it off, I am sure he would do better – *do* try it," she said persuasively, "I would be very glad if you did."

"Well, well", said Jakes, with a short laugh, "anything to please a lady. How far would you wish it down, ma'am?"

"Quite down, give him his head altogether."

The rein was taken off, and in a moment I put my head down to my very knees. What a comfort it was! Then I tossed it up and down several times to get the aching stiffness out of my neck.

"Poor fellow! that is what you wanted," said she, patting and stroking me with her gentle hand. 'And now if you will speak kindly to him and lead him on, I believe he will be able to do better."

Jakes took the rein – "Come on, Blackie." I put down my head, and threw my whole weight against the collar. I spared no strength; the load moved on, and I pulled it steadily up the hill, and then stopped to take breath.

The lady had walked along with us. She stroked and patted my neck, as I had not been patted for a long time.

"You see he was quite willing when you gave him the chance. I am sure he is a fine-tempered creature, and I dare say has known better days. You won't put that rein on again, will you?" for he was just going to hitch it up on the old plan.

"Well, ma'am, I can't deny that having his head has helped him up the hill, and I'll remember it another time – and thank you, ma'am – but if he went without a bearing rein, I should be a laughingstock; it is the fashion, you see."

"Is it not better," she said, "to lead a good fashion, than to follow a bad one? A great many gentlemen do not use bearing reins now. Our carriage horses have not worn them for fifteen years, and work with much less fatigue than those who have them. Besides," she added, in a very serious voice, "we have no right to distress any of God's creatures without a very good reason. We call them dumb animals, and so they are, for they cannot tell us how they feel, but they do not suffer less because they have no words. But I must not detain you now. I thank you for trying my plan with your good horse, and I am sure you will find it far better than the whip. Good day," and with another soft pat on my neck she stepped lightly across the path, and I saw her no more.

"That was a real lady," said Jakes. "She spoke just as polite as if I was a gentleman, and I'll try her plan – uphill, at any rate." I must do him the justice to say that he let my rein out several holes, and going uphill after that he always gave me my head; but the heavy loads went on. Good feed and fair rest will keep up one's strength under full work, but no horse can stand against overloading, and it pulled me down so badly, that a younger horse was bought in my place. I also suffered at this time from a badly lighted stable. There was only one very small window at the end, and the consequence was that the stalls were almost dark. Besides the depressing effect this had on my spirits, it very much weakened my sight, and when I was suddenly brought out of the darkness into the glare of daylight it was very painful to my eyes. Several times I stumbled over the threshold, and could scarcely see where I was going.

I believe, had I stayed there very long, I should have become half blind and that would have been a great misfortune, for I have heard men say, that a stone-blind horse was safer to drive than one which had imperfect sight, as it generally makes them very timid. However, I escaped without any permanent injury to my sight, and was sold to a large cab owner.

47. Hard Times

I SHALL never forget my new master; he had black eyes and a hooked nose, his mouth was as full of teeth as a bulldog's, and his voice was as harsh as the grinding of cart wheels over gravel stones. His name was Nicholas Skinner, and I believe he was the same man that poor Seedy Sam drove for.

Much as I had seen before, I never knew until now the utter misery of a cab horse's life. Skinner had a set of cabs and a set of drivers. He was hard on the men, and the men were hard on the horses. In this place we had no Sunday rest, and it was in the heat of summer.

Sometimes on a Sunday morning, a party of five men would hire the cab for the day and I had to take them ten or fifteen miles out into the country, and back again; never would any of them get down to walk up a hill, unless indeed, when the driver was afraid I would not manage it, and sometimes I was so fevered and worn that I could hardly touch my food. How I used to long for the nice bran mash with nitre in it that Jerry used to give us on Saturday nights in hot weather, that used to cool us down and make us so comfortable. Then we had two nights and a whole day for unbroken rest, and on Monday morning we were as fresh as young horses again; but here, there was no rest, and my driver was just as hard as his master. He had a cruel whip with something so sharp at the end that it sometimes drew blood, and he would even whip me under the belly, and flip the lash out at my head.

My life was now so utterly wretched that I wished I might drop down dead at my work, like Ginger, and be

out of my misery – and one day my wish very nearly came to pass.

I went on the stand at eight in the morning, and had done a good share of work, when we had to take a fare to the station. A train was just expected in, so my driver pulled up at the back of some of the outside cabs, to take the chance of a return fare. It was a very long train, and our cab was called for. There was a party of four; a noisy, blustering man with a lady, a little boy, and a young girl, and a great deal of luggage. The lady and the boy got into the cab, and while the man ordered about the luggage, the young girl came and looked at me.

"Papa," she said, "I am sure this poor horse cannot take us and all our luggage so far, he is so very weak and worn out; do look at him."

"Oh! he's all right, miss," said my driver. "He's strong enough."

The porter, who was pulling about some heavy boxes, suggested to the gentleman that as there was so much luggage, he might take a second cab.

"Can your horse do it, or can't he?" said the blustering man.

"Oh! he can do it all right, sir; he could take more than that." And he helped to haul up a box so heavy that I could feel the springs go down.

"Papa, papa, do take a second cab," said the young girl in a beseeching tone. "I am sure this is very cruel."

"Nonsense, Grace, get in at once, and don't make all this fuss. A pretty thing it would be if a man had to examine every cab horse before he hired it – the man knows his own business of course. There, get in – and hold your tongue!"

My gentle friend had to obey; and box after box was

dragged up and lodged on the top of the cab, or settled
by the side of the driver. At last all was ready, and with
his usual jerk at the rein, and slash of the whip, he drove
out of the station.

I got along fairly well until we came to Ludgate Hill,
but there the heavy load and my own exhaustion were too
much. I was struggling to keep on, goaded by constant
chucks of the rein and use of the whip, when, suddenly –
I cannot tell how – my feet slipped from under me, and I
fell heavily to the ground on my side. The force with
which I fell seemed to beat all the breath out of my body.
I had no power to move, and I thought now I was going
to die. I heard a sort of confusion around me and loud
angry voices, but it was all like a dream. I thought I
heard that sweet pitiful voice saying, "Oh! that poor
horse! it is all our fault." Some one came and loosened
the throat strap of my bridle, and undid the traces which
kept the collar so tight upon me. Some one said, "He's dead,
he'll never get up again." Then I could hear a policeman
giving orders, but I did not even open my eyes; I could
only draw a gasping breath now and then. Some cold
water was thrown over my head, and some cordial was
poured into my mouth, and something was put over me.

I cannot tell how long I lay there, but I found my life
coming back, and a kind-voiced man was patting me and
encouraging me to rise. After some more cordial had
been given me, and after one or two attempts, I staggered
to my feet, and was gently led to some stables which were
close by. Here I was put into a well-littered stall, and some
warm gruel was brought to me, which I drank thankfully.

In the evening I was sufficiently recovered to be led
back to Skinner's stables, where I think they did the best
for me they could. In the morning Skinner came with a

farrier to look at me. He examined me very closely, and said,

"This is overwork more than disease, and if you could give him a rest for six months, he would be able to work again; but now there is not an ounce of strength in him."

"Then he must go to the dogs," said Skinner. "I have no meadows to nurse sick horses in – he might get well or he might not; that sort of thing don't suit my business. My plan is to work 'em as long as they'll go, and then sell 'em for what they'll bring. at the slaughterhouse or elsewhere."

"If he was broken-winded," said the farrier, "you had better have him killed out of hand, but he is not. There is a sale of horses coming off in about ten days; if you rest him and feed him up, he may pick up, and you may get more than his skin is worth, at any rate."

Upon this advise Skinner, rather unwillingly I think, gave orders that I should be well fed and cared for, and the stable man, happily for me, carried out the orders with a much better will than his master had in giving them. Ten days of perfect rest, plenty of good oats, hay, bran mashes, with boiled linseed mixed in them, did more to get up my condition than anything else could have done. Those linseed mashes were delicious, and I began to think, after all, it might be better to live than go to the dogs. When I was taken to the sale, a few miles out of London, I felt that any change from my present place must be an improvement, so I held up my head, and hoped for the best.

48. Farmer Thoroughgood and his Grandson Willie

AT this sale, of course, I found myself in company with the old broken-down horses – lame, broken-winded, old, and some that I am sure it would have been merciful to shoot.

Many of the buyers and sellers looked not much better off than the poor beasts they were bargaining about. There were poor old men, trying to get a pony for a few pounds, that might drag about some little wood or coal cart. There were poor men trying to sell a worn-out beast for two or three pounds, rather than have the greater loss of killing him. Some of them looked as if poverty and hard times had hardened them all over; but there were others that I would have willingly used the last of my strength in serving – poor and shabby, but kind and human, with voices that I could trust. There was one tottering old man who took a great fancy to me, and I to him, but I was not strong enough.

I noticed a man who looked like a gentleman-farmer, with a young boy by his side; he had a broad back and round shoulders, a kind, ruddy face, and he wore a broad-brimmed hat. When he came up to me and my companions, he stood still, and looked at us sympathetically. I saw his eye rest on me; I had still a good mane and tail, which did something for my appearance. I pricked my ears and looked at him.

"There's a horse, Willie, that has known better days."

"Poor old fellow!" said the boy. "Do you think, grandpapa, he was ever a carriage horse?"

"He might have been anything when he was young; look at his nostrils and his ears, the shape of his neck and shoulders; there's a deal of breeding about that horse." He put out his hand and gave me a kind pat on the neck. I put out my nose in answer to his kindness. The boy stroked my face.

"Poor old fellow! see, grandpapa, how well he understands kindness. Could not you buy him and make him young again, as you did with Ladybird?"

"My dear boy, I can't make all old horses young. Besides, Ladybird was not so much old, as run down and badly used."

"Well, grandpapa, I don't believe that this one is old; look at his mane and tail. I wish you would look into his mouth, and then you could tell. Though he is so very thin, his eyes are not sunk like some old horses."

The old gentleman laughed. "Bless the boy! he is as horsey as his old grandfather."

The man who had brought me for sale now put in his word.

"The young gentleman's a real knowing one, sir. Now the fact is, this horse is just pulled down with overwork in the cabs. He's not an old one, and the horse doctor says that a six months' rest would set him right up, as his wind was not broken. I've had the tending of him these ten days past, and a gratefuller, pleasanter animal I never met with, and it would be worth a gentleman's while to give a five-pound note for him, and let him have a chance. I'll be bound he'd be worth twenty pounds next spring."

The old gentleman laughed, and the little boy looked up eagerly.

"Oh! grandpapa, did you not say the colt sold for five pounds more than you expected? You would not be poorer if you did buy this one."

The farmer slowly felt my legs, which were much swelled and strained, then he looked at my mouth: "Thirteen or fourteen, I should say. Just trot him out, will you?"

I arched my poor thin neck, raised my tail a little, and threw out my legs as well as I could, for they were very stiff.

But the old gentleman must have liked what he saw for he bought me for five pounds and had me taken to the inn.

The boy could hardly control his delight, and the old gentleman seemed to enjoy his pleasure. I had a good meal at the inn, and was then gently ridden home by a servant of my new master's and turned into a large meadow with a shed in one corner of it.

Mr. Thoroughgood – for that was the name of my benefactor – gave orders that I should have hay and oats every night and morning, and the run of the meadow during the day, and told Willie to take charge of me.

The boy was proud of his charge, and undertook it in all seriousness. There was not a day when he did not pay me a visit; sometimes giving me a bit of carrot, or something good, or sometimes standing by me while I ate my oats. He always came with kind words and caresses, and of course I grew very fond of him. He called me Old Crony, as I used to come to him in the field and follow him about. Sometimes he brought his grandfather, who always looked closely at my legs.

"He is improving so steadily," said Mr. Thoroughgood, "that I think we shall see a change for the better in the spring."

The perfect rest, the good food, the soft turf, and gentle exercise, soon began to tell on my condition and my spirits. I had a good constitution from my mother, and I was never strained when I was young, so that I had a better chance than many horses, who have been worked before they came to their full strength. During the winter my legs improved so much that I began to feel quite young again. The spring came, and one day in March Mr. Thoroughgood determined that he would try me in the phaeton. I was well pleased, and he and Willie drove me a few miles. My legs were not stiff now and I did the work with perfect ease.

"He's growing young, Willie; we must give him a little gentle work now, and by midsummer he will be as good as Ladybird. He has a beautiful mouth, and good paces, they can't be better."

"Oh! grandpapa, how glad I am you bought him!"

"So am I, my boy, but he has to thank you more than me. We must now be looking out for a quiet gentle place for him, where he will be valued."

49. My Last Home

ONE day during this summer the groom cleaned and dressed me with such care that I thought some new change must be at hand. He trimmed my fetlocks and legs, passed the tarbrush over my hoofs, and even parted my forelock. I think the harness had an extra polish.

"I hope the ladies take to him," said the old gentleman.

"We can but try."

We came to a pretty house, with a lawn and shrubbery at the front, and a drive up to the door. Willie rang the bell, and Mr. Thoroughgood went into the house. In about ten minutes he returned, followed by three ladies. Miss Lavinia, a tall, pale lady, wrapped in a white shawl, leaning on a younger lady, with dark eyes and a merry face; the other, a very stately-looking person, was Miss Blomefield. They all came and looked at me and asked questions. The younger lady – that was Miss Ellen – took to me very much; she said she was sure she would like me, I had such a good face. Miss Lavinia said that she would always be nervous in riding behind a horse that had once been down, as I might come down again.

"Many good horses," said Mr. Thoroughgood, "have had their knees broken through the carelessness of their drivers, without any fault of their own, and from what I see of this horse, I would say that is his case. Why not have him on trial, and then your coachman will see what he thinks of him."

"You have always been such a good adviser to us," said the stately lady, "that your recommendation would go a long way with me, and if my sister Lavinia sees no objection, we will accept your offer of a trial, with thanks."

It was then arranged that I should be sent for the next day.

In the morning a smart-looking young man came for me. At first he looked pleased, but when he saw my knees, he said in a disappointed voice:

"I didn't think, sir, you would have recommended my ladies a blemished horse like that."

"Handsome is as handsome does," said my master; "you are only taking him on trial, and I am sure you will do fairly by him, young man, and if he is not as safe as any horse you ever drove, send him back."

I was led home, placed in a comfortable stable, fed, and left to myself. The next day, when my groom was cleaning my face, he said,

"That is just like the star that Black Beauty had, he is much the same height too; I wonder where he is now."

A little further on he came to the place in my neck where I was bled, and where a little knot was left in the skin. He started, and began to look me over carefully, talking to himself.

"White star in the forehead, one white foot on the off side, this little knot just in that place" – then looking at the middle of my back – "and as I am alive, there is that little patch of white hair that John used to call 'Beauty's threepenny bit'. It *must* be Black Beauty! Why, Beauty! Beauty! do you know me? little Joe Green, that almost killed you?" And he began stroking and patting me as if he was quite overjoyed.

I could not say that I remembered him, for now he was a strapping young fellow, with a man's voice, but I was sure he knew me, and that he was Joe Green, and I was very glad. I put my nose up to him, and tried to say that we were friends. I never saw a man so pleased.

"Give you a fair trial! I should think so indeed! I wonder who the rascal was that broke your knees, my old Beauty! You must have been badly served somewhere. Well, it won't be my fault if you haven't good times of it now. I wish John Manly was here to see you."

In the afternoon I was put into a low Park chair and Miss Ellen tried me, and Green went with her. I soon found that she was a good driver, and she seemed pleased with my paces. I heard Joe telling her that he was sure I was Squire Gordon's old Black Beauty.

When we returned, the other sisters came out to hear how I had behaved. She told them what she had just heard, and said,

"I shall certainly write to Mrs. Gordon, and tell her that her Black Beauty has come to us. How pleased she will be!"

After this I was driven every day for a week or so, and as I appeared to be quite safe Miss Lavinia at last ventured out in the small close carriage. After this it was quite decided to keep me and call me by my old name of "Black Beauty".

I have now lived in this happy place a whole year. Joe is the best and kindest of grooms. My work is easy and pleasant, and I feel my strength and spirits all coming back again. Mr. Thoroughgood said to Joe the other day:

"In your place he will last until he is twenty years old – perhaps more."

Willie always speaks to me when he can, and treats me as his special friend. My ladies have promised that I shall never be sold, and so I have nothing to fear; and here my story ends. My troubles are all over, and I am at home; and often before I am quite awake, I imagine I am still in the orchard at Birtwick, standing with my old friends under the apple trees.